Praise for the Destination: Desire series

"I loved this amazing, emotional love story... A tear or two became commonplace during some intense scenes. In Ms. Jordan's talented hands, the characters evolved naturally and realistically, flaws and all."
-Harlequin Junkie Reviews

"5 stars. My favorite in the series so far. I just loved the back story of this couple and it's just a different twist on a romance. Loved it!" *-Kristi Simonsen*

"This is an well written story, where you get invested in the characters and root for them to have their HEA...I cannot wait to see what comes next in this series. 5 stars" *-Gigi Staub*

"This was a fabulous story with great characters... one of the best I've read this year. I LOVED this." *-Jennifer McKenzie*

A LITTLE SINFUL

DESTINATION: DESIRE
BOOK 1

C. JORDAN

CJ BOOKS

Book cover by James, GoOnWrite.com

This work was originally published as an e-book in © 2013, with a second edition in © 2024.

First print edition 2025

contents

Dedication

For the Professor Moriarty and the Mad Madam M. Because you are who you are. Indispensable.

For my fellow writers in the *Ooh! Shiny!* group—Loribelle Hunt, Dayna Hart, Kate Pearce, Patti O'Shea, R.F. Long, and Lee Bross. Because you keep me sane by being as insane as I am.

For Monica Murphy and Shelli Stevens. Monica for having bats and boars and pizza at her house, and letting me have a sleepover. And Shelli for dragging Monica and me all over Disneyland and then making us hike all the way back to the hotel after the park closed. There's never been a cuter drill sergeant in the happiest place on earth. Good times!

Last, but never least, for the ladies on my street team. You're the best! A special shout out to KittyKelly, who always keeps me on track with promo, and Ursula Avery, who donated her name to a character in this book. Thanks bunches!

CHAPTER ONE

Half Moon Bay, California

"Come on, Anne. The least you can do is ask her for me. She'll listen to you." Finn Walsh offered his most winning smile, but his colleague gave him a dubious glance.

"Why exactly would I help you get in my friend's pants?" Anne Kirby snorted, bending her long limbs into a stretch as she and Finn warmed up to start the day. Teaching physical education at a middle school kept them running. "Besides, Meg turned you down the one time you asked her out."

Yeah, she had. Finn winced. "I don't want to get in her pants."

Anne straightened and stared at him. "Right, I believe that one. You want to date Meg, but you don't want to do her."

He lowered himself to the wood gym floor and grabbed the toe of his sneaker to flex his calf. Meg's heart-shaped face filled his mind. Brunette curls he wanted to tangle his fingers in, eyes that were an impossible shade of storm cloud gray. She wasn't tall or short, just average, but she had curves in all the right places. Her ass, especially. Tight, round and perfect. He wanted to get his hands on it. Hell, he wanted to get his hands on all of her as often as humanly possible. But if it were just about getting laid, he could find a woman easily. No, he wanted Meg specifically. "Okay, I don't *only* want to get in her pants."

"That's a little more believable." Anne smiled when the school bell rang. Within a few minutes, gangly tweens began trudging past them into the changing room.

"I mean it." Finn waved to a few of his students, then picked himself up off the floor. "I like her, Anne. She turned me down because she thinks it's a bad idea to date coworkers. She never said she wasn't interested in me."

After crossing her arms, Anne shrugged. "She's being smart about it. We had an ugly breakup between two teachers a few years back, before you came to HMB. The memory for those of us who were here is still pretty fresh and really harsh. I don't know if I'd date another teacher, either. When it goes sour—"

"*If*, not when. It doesn't have to go sour." Usually, he wasn't one to fish in the work dating pool either, but for Meg he'd make an exception. She taught history—was quiet, smart, and drew him like a magnet. Seeing her was his best reason to show up for staff meetings. He liked being around her, liked her considered approach to every controversy that came up at work. She wasn't outspoken and ready to jump into the fray like Anne, but when she offered an opinion, everyone listened. Everything about Meg appealed to Finn. There was huge potential between them, potential for something that could actually last. He knew it without any doubts.

"Please. There are two options with relationships. They either go happily ever after or they go sour." Anne arched an incredulous brow. "You're saying you want happily ever after without going on a single date with her?"

Maybe. He clamped his lips shut on that answer, shock spiking through him. He'd known his interest was serious, but his reaction to the question floored him. Swallowing hard, he focused on Anne. "Even if things end, it doesn't have to be ugly. I'm still friends with a couple of women I used to date. I'm not a love 'em and leave 'em douche bag. You'd have heard about it if I were—Half Moon Bay isn't that big a city."

Running a hand through her short red hair, she sighed. "True enough."

"I just need her to see me outside of work. She's on autopilot, shoving me into the 'no way' category without giving me a chance. Getting away from our everyday interactions here might just shake her out of that." He held up his hands in a placating gesture. "I'm not going to take advantage of her or force her into anything she doesn't want. I just want her to really consider if she does want me. She's not doing that now."

The few times he'd caught Meg looking at him, he could tell she wasn't unaffected. She'd just made the rational decision that dating him was a bad idea. He needed to change her mind. He needed her to see him as a man and not just a fellow teacher.

Anne narrowed her eyes. "You swear you won't get her drunk in Vegas to sleep with her?"

School would let out for spring break on Friday, and a group of teachers was heading for Las Vegas for a week of rest and relaxation. Or partying, gambling, and booze—whatever they preferred. Finn had latched on to the idea that this was the perfect way to get Meg away from work without her having to agree to go out with him. A week to wear down her defenses was just what he needed. But without Anne to prod her, she'd never go on that kind of trip. Twisting Anne's arm was his first order of business.

"Yeah, because sloppy drunk women are so hot." He rolled his eyes. "Try to remember I'm not a douche bag. I wouldn't do that to anyone, least of all a woman I like." Maybe more than liked, but he kept that to himself. He'd never get the chance to figure out what might come of his jonesing for Meg if he didn't get her to spend time with him.

The squeak of tennis shoes echoed in the wide gymnasium as students flooded out of the changing rooms. Anne blew out a breath. "All right, I'll ask her. Just ask. If she says no, that's it. We're meeting up for dinner tonight, so..."

He grinned wryly. "Don't mention me when you ask."

"I won't." She laughed.

"Thanks."

"You owe me one." Lifting a whistle to her lips, she let out a shrill blast and her class obediently began to line up for roll call. "I think my class needs to run the mile today."

"Have fun, sadist." He motioned to his students and they lined up as well. Grabbing his clipboard from where it lay on the bleachers, he shook his head at her.

She jogged in place for a moment. "I can only be nice to so many people in one day. You just used up my quota."

"Lucky me."

A light rain fell as Meg Phillips hurried across Main Street toward the Moonside Café. The salty scent of the Pacific Ocean blew on the breeze, and she drank in the familiar smell. If she were a few blocks closer, she'd be able to hear the thundering crash of waves. Typical early spring day on the California coast, and she loved it. The mist would make her curly hair a frizzy mess, but who cared? She had no one to impress. She stepped inside the café, brushed a wayward tendril out of her eyes, and glanced around.

"Over here!" Anne waved from a table by the window. Their friend Karen sat beside her, already cradling a cup of coffee between her hands.

"Julie's just locking up at Purl Moon and then she'll be over," Karen said, and her expression softened. "It's been a rough day for her."

Sympathy squeezed inside of Meg. Yeah, those kinds of days happened after you lost someone you loved. Julie's great aunt Eloise had passed away a few months before, leaving Julie to run her yarn and fiber arts store. The foursome had been friends since elementary school, so they knew how much Julie and Auntie Eloise had adored each other. Her death had hit Julie hard. Working at Purl Moon had to keep the memories fresh. Eventually that might be a good thing, but right now it meant their friend had a lot of rough days.

"Well, we'll cheer her up." Meg slid into a chair across from Karen, who was the only married one in their little group. "How's the hubby?"

"Tate's working, as usual." She offered up a wry smile, her blond brows arching. "Someday, I'm going to get that man to take me on a nice, long vacation. Where he has no access to his cell phone or internet. Heaven."

Anne leaned forward, sudden interest lighting her face. "Yeah, it's important to take some time off and enjoy yourself once in a while. Right, Meg?"

Something in her friend's tone made her wary, and Meg narrowed her gaze. "Yeah, why?"

"Because a bunch of the HMB teachers are going to Vegas for spring break, and you're coming with us." The redhead's smile was sunny and appeared far too innocent.

Yeah, right. As if Anne could ever pull off innocent. Not since the third grade, anyway. Meg snorted a laugh. "Ha!"

"Come on," her friend cajoled. "When's the last time you got out of town? Be honest."

She opened her mouth, closed it again. Enough time had passed that she honestly didn't remember. She brushed an invisible speck of lint off her sleeve. "I prefer staycations."

"You can curl up with a book in Las Vegas as easily as you can here." Anne gestured to the gloomy day outside. "You'd even get a little sun in the process."

Karen tilted her head, the sweep of her blond bob brushing her cheek. "You are looking a little pale."

Sticking her tongue out, Meg folded her arms. "Thanks, that's flattering."

"The truth hurts," Anne shot back.

"It's only a week, Meg." Karen picked up the refrain, and Meg had to wonder if the two had planned this before she'd arrived. She wouldn't put it past them. Friends could be wily like that. Karen gestured to her partner in crime. "And Anne will be there—some of the other teachers too, so you won't be alone. A little socializing would be good for you."

"It's not like I'm a hermit. I get out of the house for work every day." It sounded pathetic, like that was the only time she ventured out, and Meg didn't want to admit that maybe it was. Other than their group's weekly dinner, she hadn't made much effort to get out lately. Damn, they had a point, and she hated it. "Who else is going?"

Anne didn't meet her gaze. "A bunch of us. Ed, Cindy, Karla, Finn, Doreen, Roger, Frank, me...and you."

But Meg honed right in on the name that had been sandwiched in the middle. "Finn's going?"

"You don't like Finn?" Sudden concern shone in Anne's golden eyes. "Has he been bothering you?"

Hot and bothered was a good description for what he did to her, but there was no way in hell Meg was telling her friends that. They'd try to push her into going out with him. She focused on the scarred tabletop. "No, no. He hasn't bothered me at all. He only asked me out the one time, and that was ages ago. It's fine. He's fine."

He was more than fine, and turning down his offer had sucked. The school might not have rules against teachers dating, but she had personal rules against it, and she had those rules for very good reasons. But she felt a twinge of regret every time she ran into him at work. She sighed. It really was too bad.

"Okay, then. It's fine." Anne waved a dismissive hand, but when Meg glanced at her, there was more than a little calculation in her expression. "Besides, they have museums and stuff you can check out, too. It's not all booze and broads. There are shows, shopping, gourmet food. It'll be fun."

"It'll be expensive," Meg groused.

"*Pfft.*" The redhead huffed. "The flights to Vegas are cheap from SFO, and we can room together and split the hotel costs."

Meg opened her mouth to continue arguing, but before she could, Julie jogged into the café, shaking rain out of her hair. "Hey, guys. What's up?"

"We're trying to talk Meg into going with Anne to Las Vegas for spring break." Karen flagged down a waitress. "And now that you're here, we can order dinner. I'm famished."

They'd been to this café enough times they had the menu memorized, so ordering was quick and the waitress brought them a round of coffee without asking.

Meg looked up. "Oh, I forgot to ask for—"

The old guy at the next table leaned over and deposited a small container of cream at her elbow. "No need. I'm done with it."

"Thanks, Paul." Meg shook her head. The wonders of small-town life. Everyone knew everything about you, including how you took your coffee.

"You should definitely go to Vegas." Julie tucked a lock of dark hair behind her ear. "Don't sit around at home alone on your vacation."

Meg gave the other woman a pointed look. "If anyone needs to get away from here, it's you."

Dark circles smudged Julie's eyes. She looked pale and...sad. It was hard to watch, but grief was hard, and nothing but time made it any easier. A wan smile crossed Julie's face. "I'm still wrapping my head around running the business. Purl Moon's doing well, but I can't leave it to go gallivanting." Her shoulder twitched in a shrug. "Maybe later this year."

"Three against one. Don't be a spring break hermit hunched over your books at home." Anne widened her eyes theatrically. "You'll turn into Quasimodo."

Meg snorted, though her mouth curved in a reluctant grin. "Fine, but one of you has to watch Hugo."

Julie and Karen groaned pitifully, but Meg crossed her arms and arched an eyebrow at them. "With melodrama like that, you'll get along perfectly with my depressive basset hound."

"The last time he was in the shop, he chewed up some very expensive yarn and then made sad puppy eyes at me. Made me feel bad when he was the one who chewed stuff." Julie held up her hands. "I can't take the guilt. That mutt is a menace."

"I'll do it." Karen sighed. "Maybe it'll encourage Tate to take me out of town, if only to escape the doggie breath."

"That's the spirit." Meg grinned, enjoying the chance to torment her friends. Hey, turnabout was fair play. But her smile faded when she realized she'd actually agreed to spend her break in Las Vegas.

Somehow, she had a feeling she was going to regret this.

CHAPTER TWO

Meg got stuck in the middle seat on the plane.

She should have known it was a bad sign. The seventh grade science teacher, Karla, dumped her rum and Coke all over Meg's white shirt and tan capris on the flight to Vegas. No amount of dabbing in the miniscule airplane bathroom had managed to get the sticky stain out or removed the stink of distillery that floated in a cloud around her.

Awesome start to the vacay.

She slumped in her seat, feeling disgusting, and cranked up the volume on her earbuds so the music would drown out the two English teachers' giggling. How had she let Anne talk her into this? How could her three best friends have conspired against her this way? She could be home with a glass of wine—in her hand and not on her clothes—reading the new Cleopatra biography, sitting in the wicker chair on her balcony with her feet propped on the railing. She clenched her teeth as turbulence made the plane shudder and her stomach flip.

Thank God this was a short flight.

Thirty minutes later, she was waiting for her luggage to come around the carousel. The flash of bright lights and jarring sounds from the slot machines made her head ache. The cacophony seemed to permeate every inch of the airport. She really should have stayed home and played a hermit—it had to be more fun than this. The rum and Coke had formed a stiff crust in her shirt, bra, and capris. All she wanted right now was a hot shower in the hotel. Her stomach rumbled loudly—a reminder that she'd been trapped in the plane during lunchtime. Food would be good too, but cleaning up and a new set of clothes came first.

She refocused on the luggage carousel just in time to see her bag go trundling past her. Leaning forward, she made a grab for it. And missed. "Crap!"

"Got it." Finn plucked the heavy suitcase from the conveyer belt as if it weighed nothing.

Of course, it had to be him who came to her rescue. The smile he gave her was enough to melt any woman's resistance and leave her panting after him. With his auburn hair, laser blue eyes, and body to die for, he was too gorgeous for words, and he clearly knew it. She stiffened her spine when he beckoned her toward him. She knew she needed to retrieve her bag, but getting anywhere near the man was a hazard to her mental health.

She wanted him. It was as simple and as complicated as that. She wanted to use his very fine body as her personal jungle gym. All night long. This kind of visceral reaction to anyone was completely foreign territory for her, but her hormones did a tango every time he was nearby, reminding her it had been a very long while since she'd made time to go on a date, let alone get laid. Turning him down last year had been hard, but dating colleagues was beyond stupid. Hadn't she seen with her own two eyes just how bad it could go?

But he was still standing there waiting for her, his eyebrows rising when she remained rooted in place and continued to stare at him.

Suck it up, Meg. While she jogged around the cluster of people jockeying for their belongings, she took a moment to be grateful the airline hadn't lost her bag. At least that had gone right. She reached Finn's side, forced herself to meet his gaze, and smiled. "Thanks for your help."

"Anything for you, Ms. Phillips." His grin was warm and far too wicked for her peace of mind. She could really get creative with that *anything* he was willing to do for her.

No, no, no. He worked at her school. He was off-limits. She knew better than to go down that road. She'd strayed down it once and that had been more than enough. Hell, it had been so bad she'd never even told her best friends about it. Did she want a repeat performance on public display? No way. She and Finn both leaned down to reach for the extendable handle on her suitcase, their fingers tangling. Just that simple contact made her breath catch. She'd never touched him before—never allowed herself the temptation.

Their eyes met, locked, and for one heady moment she thought he might kiss her. Warmth spiraled deep inside her at the very idea and settled low in her belly. He still held her hand when they straightened, his palm rough with calluses that stimulated her softer flesh. She licked her lips, tried to come up with something to say, but her wits had deserted her. The intent focus of his gaze moved to her mouth, and his fingers tightened on hers.

She couldn't prevent the way her body reacted—her nipples beading, her body heating with insidious need. "Finn, I..."

Anne chose that moment to hustle up to them, luggage in tow. Meg jerked her hand away from Finn and took the handle on her bag while Anne started talking. "Oh, good, you have your stuff. Karla's already hitting the slots, can you believe it?"

"Yes," Finn and Meg echoed at the same time. He chuckled, slinging a huge backpack onto his shoulders. It looked beaten up, as if he'd hiked across some rough terrain. He had the well-toned body to make the idea believable.

Meg plucked at her stained, gummy shirt and a waft of alcohol hit her nose. "Let's round her up and catch the shuttle. I'm ready to get to Caesars Palace. Now."

It took bribing Karla with a round of drinks to get her off the slots and into the van. Then Ed, the eighth grade science teacher, broke out the flask of whiskey, passed it around, and they had a party shuttle to the hotel. When Ed handed the flask to the English gigglers, he managed to slosh some of the booze onto Meg. Seriously, it was *Teachers Gone Wild*, and the lushes were aiming for her. Rum, Coke, and whiskey. Great. Just great. Meg clenched her fists and told herself she was a non-violent person as the amber liquid spread across her chest and oozed between her breasts. She glared at Anne, who flinched and turned to flirt outrageously with the shuttle driver, presumably so she didn't have to talk to Meg.

After they arrived, it took ten minutes to pry Anne away from the guy. She'd scored his number and a date for that night, and by then the rest of the teachers had staggered into Caesars Palace to check in for the week. They'd scattered when Meg and Anne finally got to the reception desk. Meg handed over their registration confirmation and breathed a sigh of relief. Soon, very soon, she would have that shower she craved.

"I'm sorry, ma'am, we don't have any more clean rooms available at the moment. Housekeeping is still working on them." The woman gave back the confirmation paperwork and offered a helpless shrug and a sympathetic smile, which turned into a slight grimace at Meg's stained shirt. "Check-in isn't technically until four p.m., but you can come back in a little while to see if anything is ready. You can leave your bags with the bell stand in the meantime."

"Okay. Thanks." Hope crumbling, Meg felt her lips actually shake. It was one o'clock. Three whole hours until she was guaranteed a place to stay.

Anne tried arguing with the woman, but Meg took a step back and turned away. What a disaster. She stank. She was covered in cola goo. *And* her shirt was still damp with whiskey—not exactly how she wanted to wander around in the Nevada heat. She really, really wanted to be home right now, where she had access to a bathroom. This vacation was a huge mistake.

Frustrated tears stung in her eyes—or maybe it was the alcohol fumes rising from her shirt.

"What's going on?" Finn appeared out of nowhere, ducking down so he could look at her face. "Meg?"

"I don't want to be here." Her voice actually wobbled when she spoke, and a flush scorched her cheeks. Emotional meltdown in front of the hottest guy she'd ever met. Yep, it really was possible for this trip to get worse. She blinked fast and glanced away. "They don't have a room ready for us yet. Looks like the rest of the group got to the ones they had."

Anne stomped up, fire blazing in her eyes. "Well, they've given us a free dinner at one of the hotel restaurants for the inconvenience, but there are apparently no rooms to be had right this second. At all. They're booked. What the hell? No rooms in Vegas?"

"It's a fight weekend. Heavyweight boxing." Finn shrugged, shoving his hands into his pockets. "Some of the guys got tickets."

"I'm going too," Anne said. "I just didn't think it would suck up all the rooms in town."

Meg spoke through clenched teeth. "Goody for you."

"I'm not one of the people going. I have other ideas for my time here." Finn's tone was so virtuous it made her snort. He looked her over and winced. "Sorry Ed got you with the whiskey, too. I was all the way in the back of the van, so I couldn't grab him in time. Why don't you bring your stuff up to my room, use my shower, and change clothes?"

Meg sighed. The promise of a clean outfit made it the most appealing offer she'd ever had. Naked in Finn's shower was weird, but she'd take what she could get. Beggars couldn't be choosers. "Sounds like a plan."

What might have been triumph flashed in his gaze, and his smile was dazzling. "Great."

Anne stepped in front of her, her expression concerned. "Are you sure you're okay with this?"

"Do you have a better option?" Meg held her arms out and gestured down at her ruined garments. "Tracking anyone else down takes time, where I'm still gross."

"True." Anne ran her hands through her short hair. "Want me to come with you or let you do your own thing?"

"I love you, honey, but as few people as possible would be awesome right now." Meg waved her off, wishing for nothing more than to be somewhere quiet. "Go have fun with Karla. Keep her from drinking and gambling her next paycheck away."

Anne grimaced. "Will do."

It didn't take long to get to Finn's room, which worked for Meg. The sooner she could shower, the better she'd feel. And she'd really love to get some lunch. "I'm starving."

"Me, too." He opened the door and motioned her into the room. After setting her suitcase on the luggage rack for her, he shrugged out of his backpack and dumped it on the end of the bed. "Once you're showered, we can find the gang and get some food."

She wrinkled her nose, unzipping her bag to root around for some clean clothes. "They're probably eating right now. After they hosed me down, the jerks. Remind me to never, ever go anywhere outside of work with this bunch again. You all seemed so normal when we were at school, but now?"

"Hey." He caught her shoulders in his strong hands, frowning at her. "Don't go lumping me into this bunch. I'm trying to help, not off partying."

Tingles broke down her arms at his touch, and she swayed toward him just a little. She tried to inject some teasing into her tone. "My hero. Thank you."

His lips curved in a small grin, but he didn't let her go. "You're welcome. I just don't want you to think I turn into a jackass who ditches my friends the second the chance to drink and gamble comes up."

"I don't imbibe much, which is probably why this makes me even crankier." She made a face. "I didn't even get sloshed and I still got sloshed all over."

Somehow, he was even closer, and she didn't know if he had moved or if she had. His heat wrapped around her, and it felt far too nice. A masculine scent filled her nose, the smell that was uniquely Finn. He dropped his forehead to hers. "I'm sorry this has sucked for you so far. Maybe I can make it up to you."

"I don't think anything could make this trip better. It was a mistake to let Anne talk me into this. They ganged up on me, Anne and our two other best friends." She shut her eyes, sudden exhaustion hitting her, and she let herself lean into his solid strength. Just for a minute. He felt good, comforting, even though it was foolish to acknowledge it.

She sighed when his lips brushed over hers. It was soft and sweet, a light caress. He sipped at her mouth, and slow heat unfurled within her. She set her hands against his chest to push him away, as she knew she should. But she couldn't make herself do it. Not yet. Her fingers itched with the need to stroke, to explore. The fabric of his T-shirt was soft, clinging to the hard planes of his muscles underneath.

He licked his way into her mouth, and she gave a low moan as his taste hit her tongue. Coffee and hot man. She coasted her hands over his chest, and he shuddered when she brushed his nipple. It beaded tight for her, an irresistible temptation. His fingers clenched on her shoulders and she found herself backed against the closed door. The feel of him—all of him—shocked a gasp out of her. Her softer curves molded to his every hard angle. His erection prodded her belly, and his kiss became a rough demand for response.

Excitement exploded inside her, a sudden riptide that dragged her under. Her sex went hot and wet in moments, an insistent craving. Undulating against him, she tried to find some relief, but the friction only increased her agony. Her nipples thrust against the lace of her bra, which chafed her sensitive flesh. He wedged his leg between hers, the heavy muscles there pressing against her sex.

Oh. God.

Moisture flooded her channel and her heart hammered in her chest. The roar of blood in her veins drowned out any other sound in the room. She arched into him, biting his lower lip and thrusting her tongue into his mouth to mate with his. He groaned, a sound of unrestrained need, and it only enticed her more. His hands bracketed her ribs, one sliding up to cup her breast. She gasped against his lips when his fingers cupped her breast through her shirt, rolling the tight tip.

She sobbed into his mouth, her hips pushing forward, grinding her nub over the hard muscles of his thigh. The subtle rocking of his body against hers managed to stimulate every single one of her nerve endings. Shoving her hands into his hair, she held him closer, kissed him deeper. She'd never been so turned on in her life, and all she wanted was more. More, more, more. When he flexed his leg, riding it against her sex, she felt the first throb of orgasm rip through her. *Yes. God, yes.* A few more seconds and she'd catapult over that edge.

He jerked himself from her arms, staggering back a couple of steps.

Shock punched through her, and she sagged against the door, her knees weak. "Finn?"

"Not like this." He shook his head. His chest bellowed, lust flushing his face. "If we ever have sex, it'll be because we're both sure we want it, not because we can't think straight. There are a lot fewer regrets that way. I never want you to regret anything we do together."

Sanity returned in slow degrees. She dragged in a breath, tried to think of something else to talk about while her body ached with unquenched hunger. "Now your shirt is stained too."

Brown splotches of whiskey had seeped from her clothes to his, they'd been pressed so tightly together. He made an impatient noise, jerked the shirt over his head, and lobbed it into a corner of the room. "There, fixed. Now, will you go take a shower?"

The sight of him bared to the waist made her brain short-circuit. Tanned skin stretched taut over pure sinew, with just a sprinkling of springy curls. He was even more beautiful than she'd imagined, and she'd imagined him more often than she'd like to admit. She wanted to lick his small, flat nipples, wanted to slide her tongue along the ridges of his abs and follow the thin trail of hair from his navel downward. His erection tented the front of his shorts, and she wanted to see that too.

"Jesus, don't look at me like that, Meg," he said, his voice hoarse.

"Go. Take. A. Shower."

Her sluggish mind tried to grope for what he was talking about. "Shower?"

His laugh was a harsh crack of sound. "Meg, I'm hanging on by a thread here. I'm not going to be able to hold back much longer. Go now or I'll take you up against the wall. We won't even make it to the bed."

That image formed so clearly in her mind, she almost whimpered in need. Him over her, in her, moving fast and rough until they both came. She wanted that so badly she shuddered with the desire, her body primed for sex. The desperation that rocketed through her was enough to shock her back to reality.

"I—I should shower." She grabbed some clothes from her suitcase and stumbled toward the bathroom, not sure if she was making the smartest or stupidest decision of her life.

"Christ." Finn flopped back on the bed, throwing an arm over his eyes. His erection was an iron bar in his shorts, an incessant ache he couldn't do a damn thing about. God, he hoped he was playing this right, because if he'd just given up his one and only chance to have sex with Meg, he might throw himself out of his thirtieth-story window.

The spray of water sounded from the bathroom. He tried not to picture it sliding in hot beads over her naked body and failed. His erection jerked and he forced himself to get up before he used his hand to give himself some relief. He grabbed his backpack, took out his clothes, put them in the dresser, and then tossed his spare shoes and empty bag into the closet and shut the door.

The shower had stopped running, but no Meg yet, so he found the remote and turned on ESPN. Anything to keep his mind off the fact that she was nude, wet, and only a few yards away. He settled on the mattress and propped himself against the headboard.

She poked her head out of the bathroom, her hair sleeked to her scalp. He could tell she was only wrapped in a towel, though he knew she'd taken clothes in with her.

He straightened. "Did you need something?"

Closing her eyes for a moment, she cringed when she finally met his gaze. "I...uh...I forgot something in my suitcase."

"Okay, let me grab it for you." He swung his legs off the bed and stood.

"No, no. That's okay, I can—"

"It's no problem." He walked over and flipped open the top of her bag. "What did you need?"

She sighed. "I forgot a bra, Finn. You don't need to get it for me."

The woman was trying to kill him. His hard-on had just started to subside and she brought on the skimpy lingerie. Swallowing, he scanned the contents of her bag and tried to keep his voice level when he spoke. "Did you want the white lacy one on top or should I dig deeper for a different one?"

When he glanced back, he saw her face had flushed bright red, her eyes were squeezed shut, and she leaned her forehead against the door-jamb, looking as if she hoped the floor might open up and swallow her whole. "The white one is fine, thanks."

The humor of the situation got to him and he hooked the bra up by a strap and strolled over to her. He couldn't help grinning impishly when she opened her eyes. "I could make so many very suggestive remarks right now."

"I'm glad you can restrain yourself, Walsh." She stuck her tongue out at him and snatched the bit of lace out of his hand, slamming the door closed while he laughed. He heard her giggling, and the sound was sweet.

At least that had broken any tension there might have been after making out. A little equilibrium was good. She stepped from the bathroom fully dressed—a shame, but better for his sanity—and forked her fingers through her hair to loosen the curls.

"Okay, food," she said. "Should we see if anybody else is free or just go by ourselves?"

Far more than he should, he liked that she spoke of them as a unit. That was what he wanted out of this week. He just had to play his cards right. He pulled his phone out of his back pocket and sent a text to Anne. *Did you guys have lunch already? Meg's clean and we're starving.*

Her reply came back a moment later, making his phone vibrate. *We're fed. Got dragged down the Strip. Go eat! Meg wanted that Bobby Flay place.*

Meg came and peered over his shoulder. "Yeah, Mesa Grill. I looked into reviews of nice restaurants after Anne talked me into coming along. Right now, I don't care about nice. I just want food."

His phone vibrated again. Another text from Anne. *Be good to my girl or I'll break your nose!*

"My friends are as subtle as a sledgehammer." Snorting, Meg went to pick up her purse and hooked it over her shoulder.

He chuckled and typed in a quick reply to Anne as he followed Meg out the door. *Duly noted on the nose breaking. Meet us at check-in at 4?*

They rode the elevator to the ground floor and Anne gave him the green light for meeting. Good, he had a couple of hours alone with Meg. This couldn't have worked out more perfectly if he'd planned it. "Anne will meet us at registration at four to get your room. There's not a huge rush now, is there?"

"No." She grinned, slapping a hand over her growling stomach. "The only rush is for lunch."

They had to weave their way through the slot machine strobe lights, the cheering and booing at the card tables. They kept going and passed under a strange indoor floating barge with what he thought might be Cleopatra's head carved into the prow, but eventually they found the Mesa Grill. Luckily, there was no wait for a table. Their server brought them bread and they dove on it like ravenous animals.

"Oh, man." Meg sighed. "This is either the best thing I've ever eaten or I'm famished. Could be both."

The bread was in tiny rolls rather than a single loaf, and every little nugget was a different flavor. He popped one into his mouth. It had a coarse corn bread consistency with a kick of jalapeño pepper. Nice. "No, it's pretty damn good bread."

"That's what we like to hear," said the waiter as he returned to the table, a smile on his face. "Can I answer any questions for you about the menu?"

"No, I think we're ready to order." Meg's cheeks dimpled when she grinned. "I'll try the New Mexican spiced pork tenderloin sandwich. With a cactus pear iced tea."

"And I'd like the ancho chile-honey glazed salmon. I'll take an iced tea too." Finn handed over his menu.

"Very good. I'll bring your drinks right out." The server took Meg's menu as well and bustled away.

She shifted in her seat, glanced around the restaurant, and looked a bit uncomfortable. "So...when we get back, the principal wants to send me to a training for—"

"Hey, none of that." Finn quickly cut her off. "We are on vacation. No talking about work. Anything else is fair game, but not work."

Time to push her even further out of colleague mode. She'd see the kiss as a lapse and try to backpedal to familiar ground. He couldn't let that happen.

He tilted the breadbasket toward her. "Have some more bread and tell me something about you that I don't know."

Appearing discomfited, she stuffed a nugget of bread into her mouth. She chewed for a moment before she spoke. "I have a dog named Hugo. He's a basset hound, and I think he needs Prozac because he has these big, sad eyes and constantly looks as if the world is ending. He sighs like a disappointed grandmother, too."

Okay, he hadn't expected that one. Snorting, he leaned back in his chair. "How did you end up with a depressed hound?"

"I went to the pound looking for a perky terrier and ended up with Hugo." Rueful affection filled her voice. She plucked up another piece of bread and waved it through the air. "He was a dead dog walking, and I couldn't leave him there to get the needle. He's a pain in the backside, but I love him."

"Sounds like my cat." He gave a low laugh.

Disbelief filled her gray gaze. "You have a kitty?"

"An enormous, mean tomcat. No one would call this beast a kitty." He had the claw marks up and down his arms to prove it every time he tried to give the tom a bath. The groomers refused to touch him anymore. "I inherited him when my mom died because he hates my dad. Seriously, he attacks on sight."

"Ouch." She arched her eyebrows. "What's this terror's name?"

"George."

"There was an evil King George in England. George III ruled during the American Revolution. Okay, the U.S. regards him as a tyrant, but I doubt he liked us much, either." She shook her head. "Sorry, history nerd tangent. I hope I never meet the evil cat."

"My George would love you," Finn protested.

"How do you know that? He doesn't love your dad."

"Because he'd be dead meat if he attacked you, and George is a master at self-preservation. Mom and Dad let him get away with it. I wouldn't." Because he wanted Meg visiting his house. Often. The cat would have to get used to it or he'd be locked outside more often than he liked. In the rain.

The waiter arrived with their meal, and there was a moment of reverent silence as they took the first bite.

"Mmm," Meg moaned, an expression of utter ecstasy molding her features. She shut her eyes, her tongue sliding out in a slow, sensual sweep to lick her lips.

Finn went rock hard at the look on her face, reminding him that he hadn't gotten to finish what they'd started in his room. Jesus, what he wouldn't give to see her wearing that exact expression in his bed.

She glanced at him and froze, no doubt noticing his hunger now had little to do with food.

He let a small smile kick up the corner of his mouth. "You're amazingly beautiful, Meg. I've never gotten hard watching a woman eat before."

A flush washed up her cheeks, heated awareness flashing in her eyes. Her gaze dropped as if she might see his erection through the table, but he was grateful for the cover. It was one thing to want her—another to embarrass himself in public.

"I...I don't know what to say. What happened upstairs was—"

"Not something we need to discuss over lunch." The last thing he wanted was to hear her tell him about it being a mistake. He took a gulp of iced tea, hoping it would cool him down. "Enjoy your sandwich, Meg. Don't mind me if I enjoy you enjoying it."

She huffed out a laugh. "Pervert."

"You're welcome." He toasted her with his glass, and then turned his attention to his food.

The sexual tension hanging over the table eased after a few minutes, and he let out a breath. His salmon was delicious, and the cactus pear iced tea was pretty spectacular.

Meg stirred when she'd finished her sandwich and was working her way through her fries. "I'm dragging Anne over to watch the Bellagio fountains tonight, and I might make her ride up the Eiffel Tower in the Paris. It's fake historical stuff, but whatever. She owes me and I'm making her pay up."

Finn noted that he wasn't invited, which annoyed him more than it should. "You know, there are things to do in Vegas that you'd really like, but you have to go off the Strip."

"There's more to Vegas than the Strip?" She widened her eyes. "What's this craziness you speak?"

"I know it's shocking, but you can handle it." He grinned. "Did I mention I'm originally from Nevada?"

She blinked in surprise, curiosity sparking in her gaze. "No, you didn't. You gave up Sin City to come to Half Moon Bay?"

Ah, she wanted to know more about him. A very good sign. The more she knew about him, the less she could relegate him to the impersonal coworker category. At least, that was what he was hoping. "Tahoe, actually, though my dad retired to Vegas after Mom passed."

"I'm so sorry." She moved as if to reach for his hand, but stopped herself, and pulled back before she made contact. "I still have both my parents, thankfully."

"Definitely something to appreciate. We lost Mom about five years ago, so I've had some time to cope." Though there were still moments of grief that caught him by surprise. He'd had one the other day when he'd called his dad to tell him he'd be in town, only to have a woman answer the phone. It had been an awkward as hell way to find out his father was dating again. He squashed that thought and focused on Meg. "Anyway, there's an exhibit I was hoping to talk you into checking out with me. Off-Strip."

"What exhibit?" She dipped a French fry in ketchup and popped it into her mouth.

"One that combines both our loves. UNLV has a space for traveling exhibits and there's one right now on the history of the modern Olympic Games. You love history and I love athletics." He shrugged as casually as possible. "We can see if anyone else wants to come, of course."

None of their colleagues would be willing to forgo the pleasures of the Strip, he was sure. Anne was the only exception. She knew the score, so there was no telling what she might do—help him out or hinder him just for fun.

He watched Meg's desire to check out the exhibit war with her seemingly ingrained wariness. The history lover in her won out, as he'd hoped it would. "Okay, we'll ask everyone. It sounds interesting."

And he'd just scored a point in their game of hearts, whether she knew they were playing or not.

CHAPTER THREE

Meg followed Anne into their room, shut the door behind them, and collapsed against it. She let a relieved breath ease out. Surviving that much time alone with Finn had taken Olympian effort. Then she remembered she'd agreed to go to an Olympic exhibit with him. Damn. Well, Anne would just have to come along as a wingman, because Meg didn't know how much longer her resistance could hold out. Not that she'd had much resistance in his room. If he hadn't stopped, they would have had sex. She'd been ruled by lust instead of logic, and that wasn't normal for her at all.

Not good.

"Uh-oh." Anne bounced onto one of the double beds, but came up onto her elbows to stare at Meg. "That's a bad look. What's wrong?"

She pinched her eyes shut, not wanting to meet her friend's gaze when she confessed the truth, but she had to talk to someone about this. She was going to drive herself crazy if she let her thoughts chase themselves in circles. "I dry-humped Finn against his hotel room door."

"Wow, that boy works fast," Anne replied, sounding almost impressed.

"What am I going to do?" Meg looked at the other woman, hating the desperate note in her tone. "What was I thinking?"

"It sounds like you weren't thinking, but that maybe you want to do him." She grinned puckishly, shrugging. "I'm just guessing here."

"No," Meg snapped. "I have rules."

"Rules are made to be broken."

"Not my rules!" Meg shoved a hand through her hair. "You saw what happened when Brandon and Regina dated. It was perfect until it wasn't and the next thing you know the police are getting called, there are restraining orders, lives blow up, and two people don't have jobs anymore." Brandon had been a friend, and she'd been there when he'd poured gasoline on his life and lit it on fire. Ugly didn't even begin to describe it. And when she thought about her secret role in the whole mess, the guilt was almost enough to eat her alive. She shuddered, her stomach jolting. "Was it worth it? I don't think so. I'm not doing that, Anne. I am not."

The redhead was quiet for a very long moment, her gaze assessing. She probably saw far more than Meg would be comfortable with. "Okay. So don't date him, just do him."

"What?" Staggering, Meg flopped onto the bed nearest the door. "You have to be kidding me. What kind of advice is that?"

Anne sat up and propped her elbows on her knees. "Hey, what happens in Vegas stays in Vegas, baby."

Meg made a derisive sound, though her hormones jangled with a sharp disagreement. They were more than happy to take any excuse to get some play. "That's ridiculous."

"Maybe, but it'd get you laid. Been a while, hasn't it?"

There wasn't a single response she could make to that one.

Anne smirked. "That's what I thought."

"Maybe he's not as interested as you think," Meg fired back, though she thought lightning might strike her for the lie. "He's the one who stopped it, not me. I should have, but he did."

She still didn't know what to make of that. He'd been aroused, but he hadn't taken the opportunity when he'd had it. Was it really because he wanted her totally on board before sleeping with her? She didn't know many men who wouldn't have taken advantage. It was...kind. Kinder than she deserved, considering she'd had her tongue down his throat.

"Did he, now?" Anne grinned. "He's smarter than he looks."

Narrowing her gaze, Meg folded her arms. "What's that supposed to mean?"

"It means I stand by my suggestion—enjoy the responsibility-free Vegas experience. Ride that man like he's your personal pony."

Another cheer from her hormones. The thought of riding Finn made her heart skip a beat. She didn't want to want a man she worked with. Not again. But she did. It was foolish and she had to keep denying herself. Clearly, letting herself be alone with him was a bad idea, so she needed to make sure that didn't happen again. Even if it meant going off on her own or hanging out with the booze crew.

"We're going to an exhibit tomorrow on the history of the Olympics." Meg leveled her gaze on Anne. "And by we, I mean you, me, Finn, and any of the others we can round up. You owe me for making me come on this trip. You are not leaving me to deal with Finn by myself."

Her friend pursed her lips. "I get why you're hesitant to get involved in any way with a coworker, but you're never going to get him out of your system unless you try him on for size. This week is your opportunity. No strings attached."

Trying him on for size sounded far too tempting. No strings attached sounded even better. She shook her head, denying herself, denying the free pass Anne offered. Brandon had thought he could get involved with another teacher and come out of it unscathed, but he'd been wrong, hadn't he?

She should learn from his mistakes. And her own.

Anne continued her persuasion campaign. "Look, you're cautious by nature, I know that. Your parents' heinous divorce only made you more cautious around men. Are you sure you're not letting their problems influence you too much? Because this is a totally different thing. You don't have to commit to more than sex."

Heinous didn't even begin to describe her parents' breakup, but Anne was right about their example making Meg cautious with commitment. She'd learned from their mistakes too.

"When do we meet everyone for dinner?" Meg set her jaw and went to unpack her suitcase. She ignored Anne's long-suffering sigh at the deliberate change of topic.

"Not until seven. You have some time."

"Good, I'm going to do a little window shopping at the fancy mall thing they have in the hotel." She unloaded her toiletries onto the counter in the bathroom. "Maybe I'll get lucky, hit a sale, and replace the clothes Karla and Ed annihilated today."

Anne bounced to her feet. "Great, I'll come with you."

D inner was riotous. Luckily, Vegas waiters knew how to handle drunken loudmouths.

Meg shook her head. When Karla swung her wineglass a little too close, Meg grabbed her wrist. "Be careful. If you ruin another outfit, I'm going to send you a bill."

The group whooped with laughter as if that were the funniest thing they'd ever heard. Meg rolled her eyes and sipped her mojito—her first drink of the day, which she definitely couldn't say for the six stooges. Roger seemed semi-sober, but Frank was listing to one side. Any second now, he was going to be lying against Finn's shoulder. Finn cast a rueful glance at Frank, then met Meg's gaze, winked and shrugged. Somehow their colleagues had reverted to college co-eds.

Finn tipped his beer to his lips and took a deep swig. She watched his strong throat work, and she wanted to slide her tongue up his neck to his ear, maybe bite down on the lobe a little. She was usually better at resisting those kinds of thoughts, but Anne's words about using this week as a chance for a no-strings fling kept coming back to her. Could she really do that? Could she, Meg Phillips, have an affair that she knew would be short-term? She'd never tried it before, never even considered it.

One thing was certain—her libido really hoped she'd go for it.

She wished she wasn't so attracted to him, wished if she were this drawn to a man that he wasn't a colleague, but she'd been wishing that for a year and it hadn't done her a bit of good. So she could take Anne's advice and do something about it, or she could continue to make wishes that would never come true. She didn't want to date another teacher, but this wouldn't be dating, would it? It wouldn't be a relationship. It wouldn't even be a potential relationship. It would just be sex.

She shook her head at herself, at her justifications. She knew it was a bad idea, but she still sought an excuse to do what she wanted. Was that so terrible? Maybe, maybe not. Until she was sure, she couldn't make a decision.

The servers stuck with the loud and rowdy party came bearing food, which caused a cheer to go up from the table. Meg laughed. She had to see the humor in the enthusiasm with which her fellow teachers unwound from work. They'd worked hard, and they wanted to play hard. It wasn't her style, but she couldn't hold it against them. As long as they kept their cocktails away from her clothes.

Her burger and fries were pretty good, and she relaxed as everyone talked about all the things they intended to do for the week. Drinking and gambling all around, the championship fight for Anne, Roger, Frank, and Ed, shopping for the girls, and Frank was also on a mission to try every roller coaster or ride on the Strip, starting with the one at New York-New York.

"Meg, Anne." Leaning forward, Karla projected her voice enough that the entire restaurant got to eavesdrop. She motioned to Cindy and Doreen. "We're hitting a strip club tonight. You ladies want to come? Naked hot guys, woohoo!"

Anne shook her head. "I have a date tonight. I'm meeting the shuttle driver for drinks at nine."

"I'm bowing out, too." Meg smiled. "You girls have fun. Don't post any evidence on social media!"

That had them all giggling, and the guys made a few ribald jokes. Meg was glad they didn't press. Some stranger rubbing his junk in her face was not her idea of fun. She could only be glad if anyone was taking advantage of the local brothels, they didn't say it out loud. There'd be no bleaching away that mental image.

Anne's phone trilled out a ring, and she leaned sideways against Meg to fish it out of her back pocket. She answered and stuck her finger in her other ear to block out the noise of the restaurant. "Hello!"

Meg felt her friend go rigid. Anne slid out of her seat to pace in front of the table as she listened. Fear contorted her features, and when she spoke, it was slowly and distinctly. "Calm down, Mom. Tell me what happened to Cami."

"Cami?" Meg whispered, and she couldn't keep the worry out of her voice. Cami was Anne's sixteen-year-old sister, the baby of the family. Meg had done her fair share of babysitting Anne's three younger sisters, so hearing the girl's name made her stomach twist into knots.

Anne leaned forward and braced her hand on the table, her face pale. "Is the doctor there? Let me talk to them. Now, Mom."

There was silence for a long moment while she listened, and Meg gripped the edge of her seat, tension ratcheting up inside her.

"Thank you, Doctor. No, I'm not staying here to wait for updates. I'll hop on the next flight home. Try to keep my mother calm until I get there. Shoot her up with Valium if you need to."

She tapped a button, and stood there for a moment, a slight tremor running through her.

Finn stood and grabbed her by the shoulders to keep her upright. His blue eyes darkened. "What happened to your sister? How can we help?" He shook her a little. "Breathe, Anne."

Sucking in a lungful of air, Anne squeezed a few sentences out. "She was in a car accident. The doctor says it's minor—she needed five stitches, has a concussion and they're keeping her overnight for observation. But my mom is freaking out and I need to be there. The girls depend on me to be the responsible one."

Truer words had never been spoken. Anne had basically raised her younger sisters because her flighty mother couldn't be counted on to remember to sign permission slips, send lunch money, or get the girls on the bus to school every day. If something went wrong, they turned to Anne.

Meg grabbed her purse and rose. "All right, let's get our things together and get home as quickly as possible."

"Yes." Anne nodded, some color seeping back into her cheeks. "Okay, let's do that. Wait, just me. You said *our*."

"I should come with you." Meg arched her eyebrows.

Anne's gaze went from Finn to Meg and back again. "No. I want you to stay here and enjoy your spring break."

"But—"

"No buts. I'll call Karen and have her pick me up from the airport. Julie can go to the hospital in the meantime and give us any updates." Anne let out a breath. "I want you to stay here and have fun, since I don't get to. Please?"

"Okay, if you're sure." Meg shook her head, knowing exactly what Anne meant when she said *fun*. She wanted Meg to sex it up with Finn. Even in distress, she was pushy.

Finn's fingers were flying over his phone, his brow furrowed in concentration. "Okay, there's a flight to SFO in ninety minutes. If we hurry, you might make it in time. I have the airline's phone number. Anne, you'll need to speak to them." His gaze speared the suddenly quiet group at the table. "Which of you is sober?"

Only Roger raised his hand.

"Great, you're in charge of making sure a cab is waiting at the curb for Anne so she can get to the airport. The cab lines here can take forever, so figure out a way around it. The rest of you take care of the dinner bill and we'll settle up later." He looked at Meg. "Can you get her stuff from your room while I help her deal with the airline?"

"Yes." Meg fished her key card out of her purse.

Finn nodded, surveying them like he was coaching a team to a win. "Let's hustle, people."

At his barked command, they rushed into action. Thankfully, Anne hadn't unpacked much from her suitcase yet, so Meg had everything back down to the lobby in short order. Finn met her there.

"Anne's printing out her boarding pass now, and she'll join us at the curb," he said.

"Okay." She let him take the suitcase from her and shivered when he laid his hand on the small of her back to usher her outside.

The chill of the desert night struck her as they exited the hotel, and she shivered again. They joined Roger at the curb, where he'd waylaid a taxi. Anne appeared, her printout fluttering in the breeze. Meg hugged her and Finn handed her into the cab.

Anne rolled down the window. "I'll text you to let you know what happens."

"Good." Finn knocked on the top of the taxi. "Now, go on before you miss your flight."

The car pulled away, and Roger sighed. "I'm going to go check on everyone else. They're probably still eating. You coming?"

"Not right now," Finn replied, and Meg nodded in agreement. She didn't want to go back. She wasn't really hungry anymore.

Watching Finn move into action to make sure Anne got home to her sister had made Meg's insides constrict. He really was a nice man. Sexy as hell *and* nice. It was an irresistible package. So why was she still resisting? She could have what she wanted—Finn in her bed—and leave out what she didn't want—a relationship with another teacher. She could try Finn on for size and not take it back to work with her. If he was willing to play by those rules, then she couldn't think of a good enough reason to keep denying herself the chance to find out how amazing their chemistry really was. She'd had a taste in his room that afternoon, and she wanted more.

The memory of Brandon's face, contorted with anger and pain, filled her mind, but she squelched it—shoved away the guilt that always came with thinking about him. This was a totally different situation. This time, she called the shots. This time, it was only about what she needed.

"It'll be okay." Finn set his hand on the nape of her neck, squeezing gently. Tingles flowed from the spot he touched, and goose bumps rose on her flesh.

"She'll keep us updated." Meg drew in a slow breath. "I won't be able to relax until I hear something. I'm going to go for a walk and watch the Bellagio fountains. They're supposed to be incredible at night. Want to come with me?"

His white teeth flashed in a smile. "Sure."

Everything that had been churning within her settled into place. Yes. This was what she wanted. The week was all she'd allow herself, but she'd savor every second—cut loose and enjoy herself.

This was going to be one fun vacation.

I t was a little chilly as they walked down Las Vegas Boulevard, and Finn saw Meg hug herself out of the corner of his eye. He debated the wisdom of sharing his body heat for about half a second before he reached out to wrap an arm around her shoulders. She didn't try to move away, but instead cuddled closer, their bodies bumping as they walked.

"Thank you for helping Anne." She tilted her head back to give him a smile. "You really like her, don't you?"

"No problem." It seemed like an odd question, but he'd roll with it. "She's probably one of the best people I've ever coached with, so yeah, I like her a lot."

The sound of Sinatra belting out "Luck Be a Lady" reached them before they passed the final overhead walkway that blocked the view of the massive fountains. Water sprayed up in huge bursts that were timed with the music.

"Oh, it *is* cool!" Meg's smile was luminescent, but they couldn't get close to the fountain with the thick crowd. Once the song ended, a loudspeaker boomed out that the next show would start in fifteen minutes.

"Want to wait for the next one?" He squeezed her closer. "Or is it too cold for you?"

"I can hang in there." She stepped forward to weave her way between the departing people and grabbed his hand to pull him along behind her. It was a tight squeeze, but he managed to make his way to the rail with her. It was gratifying when she leaned into him. "You're warm."

He slid his arm around her again. "You're welcome."

Laying her head on his shoulder, she chuckled, and it was pretty damn sweet. He liked the feel of her against him. He'd like it to be in a more sexual situation, but this was good too. At the moment, he was happier about a cold night than he'd ever been before.

They stayed like that for several minutes, just resting against each other. She stirred. "Can I ask you something?"

"Sure," he responded, though a bit of wariness surfaced in his mind. Whenever a woman prefaced a question like that, it tended to be weird or awkward or both.

"Why haven't you ever asked Anne out? You said you like her, so..."

And *that* one fell into the both weird and awkward group. Fantastic. There went his buzz. "She's just a friend."

"So, what, you don't think she's pretty?" She frowned at him, as if a negative response would offend her personally. This defined a no-win situation.

He blew out a breath, trying to find an answer that would not get him busted and derail his plans for the week. "She's very pretty, but I don't ask out every pretty woman I meet. Pretty isn't the only thing I'm interested in, and there's just nothing there with Anne and me. We're friends and that's all we'll ever be." Then a horrifying thought occurred to him, a wrench he really didn't want thrown in the works. "Why? Is this your way of telling me Anne is interested in me?"

"No!" She burst out loudly enough that the people around them turned to look. She cleared her throat and lowered her voice. "No. She's never mentioned it, anyway, and Anne usually does the asking if the guy doesn't get to it fast enough for her. I think you'd know."

He chuckled. "Yeah, that sounds like Anne. What did you say? Subtle as a sledgehammer?"

"Right." She laughed, warmth in her tone. "I just...wasn't sure if asking me out was standard operating procedure for you. Like you swing at every pitch until there's a hit." She made a pained face, rushing to continue before he could speak. "That sounded worse than I meant it. I'm sorry. Forget I asked."

Women were insane. All of them. He loved them for it, but he would never understand it. He had to work to keep the smile off his face. "I don't swing at every pitch. Or ask out every pretty woman. I haven't asked out all of your friends or every available teacher at school—I'm sure you'd have heard about it if I did."

"Probably." She nodded.

The opening chords of "Singin' in the Rain" poured from the speakers, and Finn and Meg were silent for a moment as the choreographed water and music show got underway. The fountains were made up of racks of spigots that swiveled and changed the direction of the spray. The bulk of the Bellagio lit the background, and streams of water arced through the air to look like a graceful dance; it was pretty impressive.

She turned her head to speak to him above the noise. "How long do you think it takes to choreograph one of these things?"

Fighting a shudder as her lips brushed his ear, he felt a rush of fiery heat. She was near enough to touch and smell, and he wanted her. He always wanted her. He swallowed, forcing himself to focus on her question. "Months, probably."

There was a short pause between songs before Elvis came on with "Viva Las Vegas".

"It's too bad Anne had to miss this. She was looking forward to a week in Vegas." Meg dropped her chin to his biceps.

"I hope Cami's really okay." He ran his hand up and down her back, enjoying the chance to touch her. "Anne talks about her sisters a lot."

He did like Anne, and Meg's question about asking her out came back to him. He realized his answer hadn't been the whole truth—just diplomatic enough to keep him out of trouble. But he'd promised himself that he'd lay it all out this week, show Meg the real him and hope she could appreciate what there was to him besides his profession. Time to put up or shut up.

"Just to be clear, when I first got to HMB, before Anne and I became friends, I might have asked her out just to see if anything was there." There wasn't. He'd figured out within the first month that while Anne was a beautiful woman, there was no sexual chemistry between them. A relief, considering he was jonesing for one of her best friends. "But I didn't, because I knew it would completely ruin any slim chance I had of dating you."

She was quiet for a moment, resting her head against his shoulder. It was nice to hold her this way, but it wasn't enough. He wanted more from her. He wanted everything. Half-assed wasn't his style.

"Finn?"

"Yeah?" He leaned a little closer to hear her over the music.

She pulled in a deep breath, then met his gaze squarely. "I'm thinking straight right now, and I really want to sleep with you."

He shuddered at that announcement, and all the blood in his brain rushed south. He cleared his throat. "I'm not in this for a quick lay, Meg."

Biting her lip, she glanced at the fountain, then back to him. "I can't promise anything beyond spring break. My reasons for turning you down last year haven't changed. It can basically be a very short affair. If—if you're willing."

This he hadn't expected. Meg wasn't a short-term fling type of woman. Not that he'd ever heard of, and he'd definitely asked around. On one hand, she was offering *free sex* for a week. On the other hand, she was offering free sex *for a week*. "Well, why don't we try this out for spring break and see how we feel at the end of it?"

"You'd be okay with that?" The look she gave him was hesitant and hopeful all at once.

"As long as we can also hang out and have it not be a straight-up shagfest..." He'd be taking a risk, betting that sharing the intimacy of sex and spending a concentrated amount of time together would make her move beyond the fact that he was a coworker and make her willing to go for something longer than a fling. But if he was going to gamble, Vegas seemed like the right place to do it. "I think I can handle it. What about you?"

She was quiet so long, he wasn't sure she would actually respond, but then she gave him the answer he needed.

"Yes."

CHAPTER FOUR

H e wanted to take his time with her. He meant to savor the experience, but the moment they got back to his hotel room, he hauled her into his arms and his mouth slammed down over hers. She met him with equal fervor, and it only fired his need. Shoving his tongue into her mouth, he groaned when she bit down lightly. Her fingers slid into his hair, holding him near, and there was nowhere else he wanted to be.

His heart hammered, his breathing picking up speed as he ran his hands over every inch of her he could reach. Soft, female curves he'd soon have stripped and spread beneath him. The very idea made his shaft harden until it chafed against his fly. Jesus, he needed to get inside her.

She reached to drag his shirt out of his pants, and the scrape of her nails made him shudder. Her hands on his flesh was beyond erotic, and goose bumps broke down his limbs. He backed her toward the bed, knowing this first round wasn't going to be as slow as he wanted, but he didn't need to drag her to the floor in his haste to mount her. His self-restraint held on by the thinnest thread. Pushing her, he watched her bounce backward onto the mattress. A little grin curled her lips—lips that were swollen from his kiss. He liked that. A lot.

She propped herself up on her elbows, lifting her eyebrows. "Hurry up, Walsh."

"You're wearing too many clothes," he pointed out. "Let's fix that."

"You first. I've been wanting to see you naked for months." She ran her tongue along her bottom lip, her gaze sliding over him from head to toe. The desire in her expression was enough to short-circuit his brain.

Toeing his shoes off, he jerked his shirt over his head. He pulled his wallet from his back pocket and fished out the condom he'd put there earlier that day, then tossed both onto the nightstand. He flicked the button on his fly and wrenched the zipper open before he shoved his pants and underwear down in one motion. She didn't bother with her own clothes, just watched while he stripped. Having her gaze on him turned him on even more. His erection was a hard arc, and he felt a bead of precome slide down his shaft.

"Now you," he growled.

But he didn't wait for her to comply. Bending forward, he yanked off her flats and tossed them aside. He slid his palms up her legs and cupped her hips for a moment before he opened her jeans, hooked his fingers in the top, and dragged them down. Her panties came with them, and that was just fine with him. The thatch of tight curls at the juncture of her thighs was almost irresistible temptation. Would they be soft or springy? He was going to find out. He was going to explore every centimeter of her body before the night was over.

She pulled her shirt over her head, dropped it on the mattress, and reached behind her to unhook her bra. Then she was nude. And in his bed. It was the hottest thing he'd ever seen. He straightened so he could take her in. Rosy nipples topped breasts that were the perfect size to fit his palms, and her skin was pure cream. Her dark hair was a sharp contrast to her pale curves. "Beautiful."

"Come here." Crooking her finger, she beckoned him near.

He shook his head. "I need to enjoy the view for a second."

"Maybe you need a little encouragement." Pressing her palm to her stomach, she slipped her hand down until she could dip her fingers between her legs. She let her thighs fall open so he could see her toy with those slick lips and tease her hard little nub.

"Holy hell, Meg." He'd known she had fire underneath that cool, calm exterior, but this was like a powder keg igniting. Boom. One second, it was harmless, the next it was lethal.

He grabbed the condom, sheathed himself, and dropped to the bed next to her. She rolled toward him until they were on their sides facing each other, pressed together from chest to knee. The feel of her against him made him groan. He cupped her breasts, and the tight tips stabbed his palms. He lifted the small globes and sucked one crest between his lips, batted it with his tongue, and shoved it against the roof of his mouth.

"Yes, yes!" Her fingers speared into his hair and she pulled him closer.

Switching to her other breast, he offered it the same treatment. She writhed against him, and the sensation annihilated what was left of his control. He skimmed his hand down her side, pulling her thigh up and over his hip. She was open to him, moaning his name, and arching her hips in offering. He sank deep within her, and the feel of her sleek channel closing around him made his heart stop.

Perfect. Absolutely perfect.

Her breath caught, her arm going around his waist. He pulled back a bit, then filled her again, the glide of his sex inside of her enough to make his skull explode. The way her gray eyes lost focus while little whimpers spilled out of her mouth did nothing to slow him down. He thrust into her, harder and swifter, picking up speed and force until the slap of flesh echoed in the room.

The mattress squeaked beneath them, their panting breaths and low groans a carnal symphony. Her breasts sliding over his chest, the feel of her soft, soft skin, was the closest to heaven he'd ever been. Hitching her leg higher on his hip, he opened her wider, shoved his length into her tight, wet sex. *God, yes.* He pushed them both to their limits, his muscles burning as he moved faster, trying to fuse their bodies together. He could feel the tension, the need, humming in his limbs and knew he wouldn't be able to hold on much longer.

She clutched him closer, her fingers digging into his skin. "Please, Finn. Please. More."

The desperate moans that fell from her lips told him she was right on the edge of coming. He wanted to send her flying. Thrusting deep—deeper than before—he rotated his hips and ground his pelvis against her.

"Oh, God. Finn!" Her nails raked down his back—a little pain to sharpen the pleasure.

The clench and release of her inner muscles around his shaft was enough to send him spinning into orgasm. It hit him with the force of a freight train, and come jetted out of him. Shudders racked his body, stars bursting behind his eyelids. He worked himself inside her sweet heat, dragging out the climax as long as possible. That she kept rocking her hips into him, increasing her own pleasure, just added to the intense rush.

"Meg," he groaned. Just her name. The only thing that mattered at that moment. Meg.

He buried his face in the crook of her neck, sucking in air as he came down from the high. It had been everything he'd fantasized about and more. And he'd had a lot of fantasies starring Meg in the last year. Hearing her scream his name and beg him to make her come was beyond hot. He wanted to do it again. Often.

It was the most mind-blowing sexual experience of his life.

T here was someone in bed with her.

The thought was foreign enough to startle Meg awake. It had been a while since she'd been in the same bed with anyone, and she wasn't used to the sensation of a man holding her while she slept, his body heat wrapping around her. It felt nice, but it was just...weird.

Ah, well. She wouldn't have time to get used to it, so she just let herself lie there for a few minutes and enjoy it. Finn was pressed against her back, his arm and leg slung over her, pinning her in place. Trying to make sure she couldn't escape? Her lips twitched at the thought.

Unfortunately, she needed to pee, so she was going to have to untangle herself in the very near future. She had no idea what time it was, but a shaft of sunshine appeared between the curtains, so she knew it was morning. The night before had been crazy. Anne had called to let them know her sister was okay, and she had taken her mother in hand, much to the relief of the hospital staff.

Then Meg and Finn had gone another round on the mattress before they'd passed out.

She waited to feel some pinch of remorse for her behavior—some morning-after regret. It didn't come. What she felt was boneless relaxation and a lack of tension that she hadn't experienced in a very long time. The buzz of endorphins that only came from really, really good sex. She'd forgotten what that could be like. A smug grin curled her lips. She didn't throw caution to the wind very often, and she doubted she'd ever make it a habit, but at the moment she didn't feel too shabby.

"Uh, Finn?"

"Hmm?" He nuzzled the nape of her neck, his stubble rasping against her skin and making her shiver.

She poked the arm that held her down. "Finn, I need to go."

That brought him awake, and his body went rigid, his hold actually tightening. When he spoke, his tone was wary. "You need to go?"

It took her a second to realize how he'd taken what she'd said. "Not go as in leave, go as in *go*. To the bathroom."

"Oh." His chuckle sounded relieved. Rolling onto his back, he let her loose.

Pushing to her feet, she grabbed her purse and hustled into the bathroom to take care of business. While she was there, she dug out a travel toothbrush she kept in her bag and got rid of her morning breath. It didn't take her long, and when she opened the door, she found Finn lounging in the doorway. Surprised, she stumbled back a step.

"Sorry. Didn't mean to scare you." His eyes danced with merriment. "I need a minute in there too. And I was curious why you needed your purse to take a leak."

"I have a travel-sized toothbrush that I always keep with me." She lifted her bag for him to see. "Sometimes I need it after lunch, but it worked well today too. The bathroom's all yours." She turned to the side to slide past him, but he pinned her against the doorjamb.

He bent down and kissed the side of her neck. "Good morning, Meg."

There wasn't a coherent response she could come up with. Her insides quivered, melted at the feel of his naked body against hers. He stroked a hand up her hip, his fingertips rasping over her flesh while he bit her earlobe. Her nipples went tight, and a shiver passed through her. She had to consciously keep hold of her purse, because it threatened to slip out of her fingers as her body went pliant for his.

"How do you feel about ordering room service and spending the morning in bed?" His voice was still a little rough from sleep, and the sound made her mind conjure up a few very naughty things they could do to each other.

Her heart rabbited in her chest, and she had to swallow before she could manage to squeeze a word out. "Okay."

"Great." He raised his head, his blue gaze burning bright as it met hers. "While I'm in here, why don't you look over the menu? I left it on the pillow for you."

After stumbling to the bed, she let her legs collapse out from under her. Her purse hit the floor with a *thunk*. Holy Jesus. She'd have thought they would have burned off some of the craving the night before, but apparently not. Heat thrummed through her, arrowing straight to her core. She crossed her legs, trying to squelch some of that longing. Being naked right now felt like too much, so she grabbed the shirt he'd discarded last night and tugged it over her head. It hung down to her thighs and sagged off one shoulder, but all the important parts were covered. Good enough. She heard the toilet flush and grabbed the room service menu. She was supposed to have looked it over by now.

Finn strode out of the bathroom, scrubbing a hand over his rumpled bedhead. She was pretty sure she'd helped mess it up before he'd gone to sleep. "Did you see anything you wanted?"

"Do you really have to ask?" She widened her eyes, waving the menu to encompass his nude body. His amazingly gorgeous, sculpted body. She had to resist the urge to fan herself.

His muscles bunched and rippled as he moved across the room. "I meant for breakfast."

"So did I." She waggled her eyebrows and tried for a lecherous look, though she doubted it was very successful.

A laugh rumbled out of him. "And you seem so quiet and sweet most of the time."

"I am, but not every second of the day." Her lips quirked and she fought a flush. "And, uh, usually not in bed."

Though she'd been a bit more uninhibited than normal last night. Apparently, he brought out the hedonistic side of her, which made her squirm a bit, but she couldn't deny she'd relished every second.

"I am so happy about that, I can't even begin to tell you." He rolled his eyes dramatically, and collapsed across the end of the bed, propping his head on his hand.

His gaze slid from her bare legs up to her wild rat's nest of hair. The inspection made her overly aware of her appearance. She forced herself not to fidget or try to smooth her unruly curls.

He tilted his head. "I like you in my shirt, but I like you better out of it."

The invitation to strip was there, but she felt inexplicably self-conscious. Not shocking, considering how long it had been since she'd gotten naked with anyone, especially someone as sexy as Finn. Who was she kidding? She'd never been with anyone as sexy as Finn. Ignoring the urge to pinch herself to make sure she was awake, she dropped her gaze back to the menu. "So, um. Maybe the seasonal fruit and banana bread thing for me. Did you need to look at this?"

"No, I saw it. I'm going for the omelet."

It only took her a moment on the phone to place their order and be promised a quick delivery. She thanked the staff member and hung up. "They said twenty minutes or so."

"Are you all right?" One of his hands wrapped around her ankle. "Are you regretting last night?"

"No!" She made a chagrined face. "No. It's just...been a while since I had to do a morning after, and I'm a little rusty on the protocol."

He rolled to his hands and knees so he could crawl up the mattress and sit next to her. "You're overthinking this, Phillips."

"I do that." What else could she say? She was a bookworm and always had been—introspection was her way. It wasn't likely to change anytime soon.

He brushed a kiss over the shoulder his shirt didn't cover and then rested his forehead against hers. "I'd already figured that out about you, sweetheart. But you don't have to worry with me. I'm not grading your post-coital protocol. I want us to relax and enjoy this week together."

She nodded, unable to avoid his gaze from this close, so she let him see the truth. "I know. It's fine...I just had an awkward moment. Really, I don't have any regrets. I promise."

Bringing his hands up to frame her face, he kissed her—the touch so gentle it made her heart tumble. She set her palm on his chest, the crisp hair there tickling her skin as she slipped her hand lower. The warm, resilient flesh just made her want to slide her fingers over every inch of him.

When he drew back and searched her face, she wanted to drag his mouth down to hers again. Then his stomach rumbled under her palm, making them both laugh.

Shaking her head, she scooted away from him a little. "Okay, we need to be distracted or we're going to end up in a really unfortunate position when room service shows up."

He shrugged to concede the point. Leaning toward the nightstand, he grabbed the remote control and flipped on the television. "There has to be something on that will entertain us both."

After pulling up the channel menu, he started scrolling through the shows that were playing. "News, no. Golf game, no. Cooking station, no. Home decorating, very big no. Oh, hey, what about *Pawn Stars*?"

"What's that?"

He stuffed a pillow behind him and sat against the headboard. "It's a show about a pawn shop here in Las Vegas. I keep meaning to go out and see it when I'm in town visiting my dad, but I never quite make it."

"And pawn shops are fun?" She couldn't keep the doubt out of her voice. She'd always pictured those places as dirty with an edge of sleaze where desperate people had to hawk their precious belongings to pay off debts. It sounded sad.

"Yes, they're fun. Just watch." His enthusiasm was undimmed by her skepticism. "This show features all the cool stuff people bring in to try and sell. They go through the appraisal process, see if the stuff is authentic and worth anything, and then negotiate a price. A lot of the things have historical value."

"Like what?" She shifted around on the mattress and settled back against the pillow beside him.

He gestured to the TV as the opening credits showed a few items featured on the episode. "Well, like stained glass windows from the Victorian period or a Babe Ruth baseball card."

Now that got her attention. She had a massive collection of baseball cards she'd inherited from her grandfather. Some of the cards were probably valuable, but she'd never sell them. The memories that came with them were priceless. "They have old baseball cards?"

"You like baseball?"

"I love baseball. My grandpa and dad are both huge, huge fans and they used to take me to games when I was little. When I was a teenager, it was the only topic my dad and I could discuss without arguing." All that arguing had cemented her vitriolic hatred for conflict.

"The teen years are rough," Finn agreed.

She huffed out a laugh. "Especially when your parents are going through a nasty divorce because your dad cheated with some bimbo named Barbie. Seriously, Barbie."

It had taken a long time and a lot of apologizing from her dad to get her back on good terms with him. At first, he'd justified and excused his behavior while flaunting his new girlfriend around town. It wasn't until the relationship had soured that he realized how badly he'd screwed up. Meg didn't think her mother had ever gotten over it—still bitter about men in general.

Finn made a little humming noise and stroked a hand down Meg's hair. "Barbie actually sounds like the perfect name for a home-wrecker."

Home-wrecker. Meg winced. She hated that word, hated how Barbie had gloated over her mom's devastation. Was there any worse kind of person?

"Sorry, I don't know why I'm telling you this." She rubbed the hem of the shirt between her fingers.

"I'm glad you did." He leaned over and kissed her temple. "Oh, look, they're doing the Babe Ruth card now."

They sat in silence for a moment to watch the process of buying and selling. Very interesting. The place didn't look gross and dingy on-screen.

When the show went to commercial, she pulled her knees up to her chest and grinned. "Baseball is so awesome. The game has such a rich history that's tied up with things like wars, immigration, and Civil Rights. It's fascinating. I even did my history thesis on the All-American Girls Professional Baseball League, which was active around World War II."

"Like in *A League of Their Own*. Good movie. It had several hot chicks." He widened his gaze innocently when she shot him a dirty look. "What? I'm allowed to notice. Besides, I like baseball too. I prefer college ball to pro though—those guys are a bunch of overpaid whiners. They're in it for the money, not the love of the game."

"Yes! Oh, my God." She threw up her hands. "I could not agree with you more."

"I take a trip over the hill from Half Moon Bay to catch the Cal versus Stanford game every year."

"Me too." It was right on the tip of her tongue to invite him to come with her, but then she stopped herself. No. That would violate her own rules, and she didn't do that.

He nudged her with his shoulder, and when she glanced at him, she knew he'd guessed what she was thinking. Amusement reflected in his gaze. "We could always go as friends."

"No. We really couldn't. You and I aren't meant to be friends." Being near him as his friend would be torture. And a lie. She'd done that with Brandon, and look how that had turned out. Another lesson she'd learned the hard way. Wanting one thing and giving something else. Better to have nothing than that endless torment. She couldn't do that to herself or to Finn. It wouldn't be right or fair.

After giving her a pointed glance, he returned his focus to the TV. "You're right. We're not meant to be just friends."

She knew he'd deliberately taken her words the wrong way, because he thought they were meant to be more than friends. There was no point arguing with him. He knew where she stood, and she knew he hoped she'd change her mind. Stalemate. But there was nothing that could change her mind, not even the best sex of her life. This...closeness between them ended when spring break did. Then things could go back to normal.

Or as normal as things ever were with their chemistry spiking off the charts.

CHAPTER FIVE

S he was a study in contradictions, and it fascinated him.

Cool, quiet, and logical out of bed. Hot, wanton, and willing between the sheets. Sweet and a little shy the morning after. If anything, last night had only steeled his resolve to change her mind. He knew she was a long way from giving in, but he wanted her even more.

The remains of breakfast were piled on a tray, and they sat together in bed watching the *Pawn Stars* marathon. It cracked him up that she seemed so enthralled by baseball memorabilia. Another surprise. But he liked just being here with her, hanging out and chatting. No pressure, no façades. The news about her parents' divorce had shed some light on her reluctance to get involved...probably with anyone, not just him. He thought there might be more layers to her resistance than he'd first imagined, no thanks to her cheating father. That would be hard to watch as a kid, and definitely had the potential to make for a wary adult.

Good thing he liked a challenge.

He reached over to run a fingertip up her arm until he touched her sleeve. "I do like you in this thing."

"I just borrowed it." She shrugged, and one shoulder of the shirt slipped dangerously low. "Don't worry, I'll give it back."

"Don't be surprised if I want it back pretty soon." He traced the curve of her collarbone, her shoulder, down the neckline of the shirt until he stroked the top of her cleavage.

Her breath caught, lifting her breasts higher. The thin cotton clearly outlined her beaded nipples, and he wanted his hands on them, wanted to suck them into his mouth one by one until she gasped and begged.

She licked her lips. "Finn."

God, he loved when she said his name like that, all breathless and wanting. It made him hard, and the fact that he was naked did nothing to hide his condition.

Her gaze dropped to his lap, and her lovely silver eyes went wide.

"Yeah." He chuckled. "I want you. Hardly a surprise, is it?"

She shook her head slowly, her gaze not leaving his erection, which jerked under her attention. Setting her hand on his thigh, she made him shudder.

"I want you, too."

It was almost too soft to hear, but his chest tightened with emotion that he couldn't even begin to name. Dipping down, he pressed his mouth to hers. She sighed, parting her lips for him, and he tangled his tongue with hers. She tasted of the fruit she'd had for breakfast and something uniquely Meg. The kiss was tender enough to make that band of emotion around his chest cinch tighter.

He cupped her breast, thumbing the tip while she moaned into his mouth. Blood raced through his veins as his heart rate sped. Her nails dug into his leg the longer he stroked her nipple, and she arched to press herself deeper into his touch. The smell of her, feel of her, was the headiest aphrodisiac he'd ever encountered. His erection ached, especially when her fingers slipped higher, her knuckles just brushing the underside of his shaft.

They both jolted when his phone blared out a ring, and he snarled. "Damn it."

"What's wrong?" The question was hazy with lust, and she swayed toward him. It made him feel just short of murderous to have to ease away from her.

"I have to get that. It's my dad's ringtone." He scooted over to the nightstand and snatched up the vibrating phone.

"Oh, okay." She ran a hand over her hair and straightened the shirt, looking self-conscious again, which made him even more furious. She hadn't been self-conscious a few moments ago—she'd been ready to pick up where they'd left off last night.

"Sorry, sweetheart. I did tell him I'd be available to talk now. That was before we started...this thing." Hell, he didn't even know what to call it. A fling or an affair just sounded insufficient, even though it was correct for what she'd claimed she wanted.

"No problem." She drew in a breath, snagged the remote control and muted the TV. "Answer the call before you miss it."

He did, stabbing the button to pick up the phone. "Hi, Dad."

"Hey, son." There was a hesitation to his voice that made Finn sit up straight.

Concern cut through the annoyance at the interruption. "What's up? Is everything okay?"

"Everything's fine. Better than fine. For me, anyway." There was a rustling sound. "The woman who picked up the phone the other day..."

"What about her?" Sudden dread fisted in his gut and he swallowed hard. Turning away from Meg, he swung his legs over the side of the bed so he sat on the edge of the mattress.

His dad cleared his throat, and there was a long, awkward moment of silence. "I'd like you to come to dinner while you're in town. And meet her."

Ah, hell. Finn dropped his head in his hand. It was strange enough that his father was dating again, but now he was getting dragged into some warped, reversed version of *Meet the Parents*? It made him feel a bit sick, thinking about some strange woman replacing his mother. But did he really have a choice? It had been years since his mom passed and there was no reason his father shouldn't date again, but Finn had just wrapped his mind around that. A girlfriend introduction was something else entirely.

"Her name is Ursula," his father continued, and Finn had to resist the childish urge to cover his ears. He didn't want to know anything about this woman. Jesus.

"When?" The word grated out of his throat and he dragged his palm down his face.

He heard his dad sigh, but didn't know if it was in annoyance at Finn's lack of enthusiasm or relief that Finn wasn't fighting him on the meeting. "You're leaving Friday, right? So, how about the night before you leave? Do you have plans Thursday?"

Finn wanted to make up some kind of plan to avoid what was sure to be a horrific experience, but he didn't. "Okay, yeah. Thursday sounds good. See you then. I have to go. I, uh, I have a friend waiting for me."

"Sure, sure," his father said, a false heartiness to his voice that made Finn cringe. God, this was uncomfortable. It didn't help that the older man seemed as ill at ease as he was.

"Bye, Dad." He closed his eyes, shaking his head. "Love you."

"I love you too, son." The words echoed with the gruff affection Finn had grown up with. "I'll see you Thursday."

Hanging up, Finn sighed. Well, there was nothing to do but get through this. His family had always been a close one, and losing his mom had devastated both his father and him. He wasn't about to alienate his one remaining parent by being petulant about the older man moving on with his life and finding someone else. Hell, his mother had even told his father to do so before the cancer had finally taken her. At the time, his dad had been adamant in his refusal and told his wife she was crazy from the chemo, but things had apparently changed.

Finn just wished he'd had a bit more warning before he'd been blindsided by this new and not particularly welcome development in his old man's love life.

He hoped there was going to be alcohol at this meal. A stiff drink, or three, was going to be in order, no doubt. "Damn."

M eg had tried not to listen in on what was obviously a private conversation, but the tension radiating off Finn was unavoidable. She could see the muscles in his back and neck grow taut. Her belly knotted, but she laid a tentative hand on his shoulder.

"You all right?" He flinched at her touch and she jerked her fingers back.

"Hmm?" He glanced over at her. "Oh, yeah. I'm fine."

Wow, there was a load of bull if she'd ever heard it. She snorted. "You don't have to tell me what's going on, Finn, but don't lie to me."

He swiveled in place so he could look at her, propping one bent leg on the mattress. "My dad wants me to come to dinner while I'm in town."

That much she'd gathered from the one-sided discussion she'd heard. What she didn't understand was why that had caused so much tension. "And you don't get along with your dad? Because you sounded like you were agreeing to go to the gallows when you were talking to him."

He forked his fingers through his hair, leaving the auburn strands in furrows. "I get along with him just fine. We visit each other several times a year."

"Uh-huh."

Wincing, he sighed. "He wants me to meet his girlfriend."

"That's the bad part?" Her brows arched. She still wasn't quite clear on the problem.

"It's his first girlfriend since Mom died. Or at least the first one he's wanted me to meet."

And there it was. The problem. "Ouch."

"I know, right?" He shook his head. "It's crazy, but it feels like I'd be betraying her by meeting Dad's other woman. Even though it's been five years and he has every right to move on." One shoulder twitched in a shrug. "My mom would have wanted him to be happy. And yet..."

"And yet it feels a little wrong to do that." The pain on his face coaxed her across the bed until she sat next to him, and leaned against his side, wanting to offer some comfort but not sure how.

He blew out a deep breath, his arm circling her waist. "Yeah."

"I'm sorry."

"I miss her. I always will." He set his chin on the top of her head, squeezing her just a little too tight. "She was an amazing mother. It's odd to think about my dad with someone else. I'll get over it. What other option do I have?" He huffed out a laugh that sounded far too close to a sob. "Jesus."

What an awful situation. Both of her parents were still alive, so she couldn't even imagine what he was going through, but the usually affable Finn being so upset broke her heart. She didn't say anything, just slid her arms around him and held on.

"Would you..." He swallowed audibly. "Would you come with me? I think it might make it easier, not to be the third wheel at dinner."

Tipping her head back, she tried to meet his gaze, but he wouldn't look at her. "Distract them with me, huh?"

"You don't have to. Never mind." He pushed to his feet, sliding out of her embrace. The smile he gave her was overly bright and totally false. "Maybe we should think about getting dressed and going to that Olympic exhibit."

"I'll go with you. To dinner."

The words were out of her mouth before she thought them through. It was unlike her not to consider things before she jumped in. Then again, she'd almost expected to regret sleeping with him when she'd woken up this morning. She was doing a lot of things that weren't like her lately.

Profound relief, disbelief, hope, and what might have been gratitude flashed across his face in rapid succession. "Really? You will?"

"Yes." Again, no hesitation—just reaction. "If me coming along helps make this easier for you, then I'm happy to come." Wouldn't she have loved someone to deflect the discomfort the first time she'd met Barbie? A friend would have been so appreciated just then, so she had some idea of what Finn was dealing with. Though without the home-wrecking part thrown in. She shrugged. "Anne would probably make for a much more entertaining distraction."

An odd expression she couldn't decipher met that declaration. "You'll be great. Thank you, Meg. Really. Thank you."

He stepped closer, caught her face between his palms and popped a kiss on her mouth. She tilted her head back, inviting more. His lips clung to hers, lingering. He tasted good. Like coffee and Finn. An addicting combination.

"Mmm. You're welcome," she said when he let her up for air. "Can your dad cook?"

He laughed. "Yes, he can. Meat and potatoes fare, but very edible."

"That's good." But reality—along with her usual careful consideration—was already rearing its ugly head.

It was, in fact, a very bad idea to go to dinner and meet his father. She might be having sex with Finn, but they really weren't friends. They'd agreed on that point earlier. She might justify it by sympathizing with the dad-has-a-new-girlfriend weirdness, but if she wasn't his friend, what was her role? It would have been appropriate for Anne to go, but Meg? Not really. So what the hell was she doing? It crossed lines and made this more personal than it really should. Meeting the parent went way beyond just sex. But she hesitated to take the offer back. When had she ever seen Finn look so insecure, so uncertain? So agonized? He was usually the king of confidence, and she found she didn't have the heart to let him down.

That should tell her something right there, but she didn't want to acknowledge it. So she pushed it aside. Not the smartest or most mature choice she'd ever made, but responsibility hadn't exactly been high on her to-do list since she'd arrived in Vegas, had it?

Finn had pretty much been the only thing on her to-do list, and she had done him. Repeatedly and in some very creative positions. And she wanted to do it again. The thought made a delicious shiver course through her.

"We should get ready to go. The exhibit awaits." This time, his smile reached his eyes, his expression warm enough to make her heart trip.

Bad, bad idea. Agreeing to this dinner was going to make him think he was gaining ground in their romantic battle of wills. Not true, she assured herself. Helping him out with his dad didn't mean she was giving in about dating him. But she didn't want to point that out. He'd see for himself.

She wanted to think about something else. Anything else. Time for some distraction, and she knew just how to get it. Letting a slow smile curve her lips, she held a hand toward him. "It can wait a little while, can't it?"

CHAPTER SIX

Mellowness filled Finn as he wandered around the Olympic history exhibit. His muscles were loose and a satisfied smile curled his mouth. Amazing sex would do that to a man. That and the sure knowledge that he was starting to make some headway with Meg. She was going to the Disaster Dad Dinner with him because she cared. She might not realize it, or maybe she just didn't want to admit it, but he had no doubts.

It gave him some hope.

Hope could be a wonderful and dangerous thing, all at the same time. He knew he couldn't assume too much from her agreeing to come with him, but there were a few chinks beginning to show in that armor of hers. He just had to keep chipping away at her resolve. Still, it felt damn good to know she cared. About him. He'd waited a year for some confirmation of that. She wanted him, and she cared.

Today was off to an amazing start, despite the call from his father.

Refocusing his attention on the display in front of him, he read a placard that discussed the life of four-time Olympic gold medalist Jesse Owens. The track-and-field champion had run in footraces against

Thoroughbred horses...and won. Finn hadn't known that. He glanced around, wanting to show Meg. She was focused on another display, her hands clasped behind her back.

"Meg, come see this," he called softly, not wanting to disturb the other people in the large room.

She held up a finger, letting him know she'd be there in a minute. Her brown curls swept forward to cover her face when she bent down to get a closer look at the glass case in front of her. The pose just drew his gaze to her heart-shaped backside. The soft sundress she wore flowed over her curves to flutter around her knees. He'd had to stop himself from sliding his hand under her skirt when they were on the cab ride over here. It would have turned her on, but she'd have probably slapped his hand anyway.

After a moment, she straightened and looked around for him. He waved her over, and she smiled as she approached. The expression was softer and more intimate than he was used to, and he liked it. Since he knew for a fact that none of the other HMB teachers were here to witness anything, he pressed a quick kiss to her mouth when she reached his side.

She set her palms on his chest, but didn't push him away, so he kissed her again, letting himself linger for just a moment longer than was strictly kosher in a public place. Her eyes were a bit glazed, and he liked that too, liked knowing he could shake her logic and make her respond.

"Was that why you called me over here?" Her fingers toyed with a button on his shirt.

"No, I wanted to show you this." He waved to the placard about Jesse Owens and gave her a moment to read it.

"Huh. I can't even imagine being able to run that fast." Her brows drew together in thought as she moved along the wall to the next display. "Did you know that baseball was voted out of the Olympics? The 2008 Beijing games were the last ones to have it as part of the core program. Since then, it's only shown up as a single appearance event if the host country wanted it."

"Where did you read that?" He glanced around at the various displays that made up the exhibit, not seeing one that looked particularly baseball related.

"Not here. I just know it." She shrugged and stopped in front of an enlarged photo of a team of ice hockey players from the USSR. "Baseball was the first sport voted out of the Olympics since polo in 1936."

"It's interesting that you like sports." It was one of the things he hadn't given a lot of thought to when he'd begun pursuing her. He'd sensed they were sexually compatible, known they had personalities that would mesh well, but he hadn't considered what interests they might share. As a physical education teacher, he was a fan of most sports, but had a few favorites—including baseball. Somehow her love of the same sport solidified the opinion that had been slowly building over the last year: they fit each other.

"Not sports in general. Baseball, specifically." She spread her hands. "My dad and gramps competed over baseball factoids and stats. There was no way to grow up in my family and avoid knowing everything."

"Who won the 1958 World Series?"

She didn't hesitate. "The Yankees."

"Who'd they play against?"

"The Braves. And the year before, it was the same teams, only the Braves won." She smirked. "Any other questions on this pop quiz?"

"Nope." He slid an arm around her waist, leaning in to brush his lips over her cheek. Damn, she smelled good—the light, flowery fragrance of her shampoo teasing his nose. He'd woken up to that scent this morning, and it was something he could get used to.

He tried to avoid considering what would happen if she didn't change her mind about them. The possibility was there, hovering like a dark cloud over everything they said and did this week. He was doing his level best to ignore it, but he had a feeling that ignoring his worries was going to get harder as the days sped by.

F inn slid his fingers into Meg's and she startled. One auburn eyebrow arched when she glanced at him. "Something wrong, sweetheart?"

"No, I just...I'm not used to this." Not from him. It was a little jarring to go from ignoring her lust for him to public displays of affection overnight. She knew none of their colleagues were near the Olympic exhibit to see anything, so there should be no problem, but it was unsettling to have her standard operating procedure with him flip so quickly. She knew she'd asked for it, welcomed it, but accepting it internally was a little less easy. A little scary.

"There's no time like the present to get used to it." He lifted her hand to his lips and brushed a kiss over her knuckles, his blue gaze daring her to pull away. Instead, she just stared at his mouth, a little quiver running through her when he nibbled on the base of her thumb. A flush heated her face, then that same heat sluiced down her body. Her muscles both tensed and loosened, readying for sex. The beat of her heart thrummed in her ears, picking up speed.

His Adam's apple bobbed when he swallowed and she wanted to put her mouth on his throat, drink in the scent of him, lick the saltiness of his skin, maybe even bite him.

"I want you," he whispered against her palm.

Her chin dipped in a quick nod. She no longer had to deny how much she craved him, at least for a few days. She waved her free hand to encompass the exhibit. "This isn't exactly the place to be able to do anything about it."

"A shame." Wickedness glinted in his gaze though, and a hint of laughter.

Releasing her hand, he bent forward and dropped a quick kiss on her mouth. She let her lips cling to his for a moment, her eyes sliding shut while his taste lingered. The sweetness of it made her heart squeeze, though she knew it shouldn't. This was an affair, so her heart should be unmoved. Or race with passion, but not trip over itself for Finn. It worried her a little, but she pushed it from her mind.

"Maybe we should go somewhere we can do something about it," she suggested. As much as she adored history, her interest in the exhibit waned under the temptation he presented.

His expression tightened with lust. "I'm ready when you are."

Desire wound through her as she turned to walk out, the feel of her dress brushing against her legs somehow heightening her need. Finn slid his hand down her back, pressing her forward. Not that she needed urging. Leaving the exhibit, she stumbled when Finn took her arm and tugged her away from the building's exit.

Frowning, she met his gaze. "Where are we—"

"In here." He drew her through a doorway and automatic lights flashed on. He shut and locked the door behind them while she glanced around and saw they were in a large single-user bathroom.

"You needed to pee before we left?"

"Nope." He curled an arm around her waist so he could drag her against him. His mouth closed over anything she might have said. She met his tongue with her own, battling him for control of the kiss.

Her hands shoved into his hair, gripping the rough silk. She shifted her torso across his, stimulating her nipples—which hardened to painful points—but the pain just increased her craving. His hands dropped to her hips, pulling her tighter to him, and the ridge of his erection rode against her stomach.

Not where she wanted it.

Tingles skittered down her limbs, and her breath sped to panting. His fingers began to gather the fabric of her skirt, and she felt cool air brush her thighs. It sent fire spurting through her and her sex clenched.

His hands curled under the band of her panties, the roughness of his calluses making her shiver. He dipped down to tease her sex from behind, rubbing his fingertip along the slick lips, circling her opening before he pressed two thick fingers into her.

"Oh, God. Finn." Her hips moved with the pace his hand set, and her mouth opened in a silent scream when he added a third finger to her channel. She pressed her face to his chest, her nails digging into his shoulders as she held on tight. "Please."

He thrust his fingers into her, deeper, then withdrew slowly, only to fill her again. Everything in her focused on what he was doing between her legs, and she could feel the building storm of orgasm gathering low in her belly. She moved her hips faster, trying to push herself over the edge. He hooked his fingers inside her, rubbing over her G-spot and it was as if a jolt of electricity speared through her loins. Her back bowed, her inner muscles fisted around his digits, and she bit his chest through his shirt.

He grunted, slipping his hand away from her. "I need to be inside you."

"But I'm so close," she objected. Her body screamed a protest at being denied what it craved so much. Her fingers bunched in his shirt, while she arched into him.

"Don't worry, I'll get you there again." He pried her hands free and spun them both, positioning her so her front was pressed against the door. She couldn't believe she was doing this—it was insane, wild. But hadn't everything about the last few days been out of character and crazy? First coming to Vegas, then what she was doing in Vegas. Madness. But she didn't want to stop. Her body was aflame, wanton and ripe for sex. The heavy rasp of his zipper sounded loud in the small room, and she heard the distinct rip of a condom wrapper. She glanced over her shoulder to see him toss the empty package in the trash and then sheath himself.

His hands curved over her hips, drawing them back until they met his. She braced her palms against the door as he rubbed the head of his shaft up and down her slit. Her chest tightened with excitement until she could barely draw a breath. "Please, Finn!"

He groaned, pushing the first inch into her. He filled her so slowly she wanted to scream. Her body demanded fast and hard. Shoving her hips back, she took him deep in one swift thrust. They both groaned, and the sound echoed. He was so wide, he stretched her to the limit. It was almost painful, but she was so wet, it made the glide totally erotic.

"Yes," she gasped. "Yes, yes, yes!"

The high pleading in her own voice shocked her. Who was this woman who sobbed and begged for more from her lover? She cut loose during sex, sure, but this was far beyond anything she normally did. They were in a public restroom, for God's sake. Turning her head, she caught sight of them in the wide mirror over the sink. Her face was flushed, her eyes glassy with lust, her lips parted as she panted. It was somewhat frightening to see herself that way, almost at the edge of feral. But it was scintillating too. The conflicting emotions became tangled with the need that Finn lit inside her. Her gaze moved to his reflection, and the desperation on his face reminded her of how he had looked the night before. His muscles flexed as he filled her, shoving deep with each push into her sex. He was a man who held nothing back, and didn't allow her to hold back either.

He reached an arm around her, his hand diving between her thighs to toy with her. All thought of their reflections dissipated as she focused on what he was doing to her body. He flicked his nail over that sensitive bundle of nerves, and she jerked in response. Her channel clenched around him, and she moaned, her eyes sliding shut so she could experience every single second of what he offered. His fingers teased her slick flesh as he pistoned in and out of her, stretching her with each pass until her legs threatened to give out. It was too much, too good, and she was moments away from orgasm.

"Finn, I'm going to—"

"Come," he ordered, pinching her nub to guarantee she obeyed.

A high-pitched cry escaped her as she clamped tight around him. He slammed deep, rotating his pelvis against her backside and a guttural groan escaped him as he joined her in climax. He pumped into her, riding her through both of their orgasms. Prickles broke down her limbs and she shuddered with every wave that rolled over her, her sex squeezing again and again.

Her knees gave way, and he caught her securely against his broad chest. "I've got you, Meg. It's all right."

When was the last time she'd felt so utterly safe with a man? Never. Her mom had felt safe with her dad and that had been one big lie, hadn't it? There was no safety in what Finn offered her—there was only lust and the rush of endorphins that made her want to believe what wasn't there. Finn might say he wanted to date her, to have something permanent with her, but she knew it wasn't true. Stiffening her legs, she forced herself to step away from him. She pulled her panties up and pushed her skirt down. She was uncomfortably wet, but she doubted anyone would be able to tell by looking at her.

He walked to the sink, cleaned himself up, and refastened his pants. "Are you all right?"

The edge of concern in his voice made her look up. She offered a weak smile. "Yes. I've...um...never done it in a public place before. It's just not like me."

"Isn't that what you wanted from this week? A little adventure before we go back to being staid old teachers?" There was absolutely no inflection to his words, so the admonishment she heard was nothing more than the bite of her own conscience.

Lifting her chin, she held his gaze. "Yes, that's exactly what I wanted."

"Then you got it." His wave encompassed the small room. Then he met her gaze. "Ready to eat?"

"Eat?" Her eyebrows arched.

"Yes, lunch. You wore me out, sweetheart. I'm famished. If you want me to keep going at your insatiable pace, you're going to need to let me carb up."

A blush burned its way up her cheeks, but she ignored it. "Well, then, let's get you fed. I wouldn't want to be responsible for you fainting under all the strain."

"Guys don't faint." He tossed a paper towel into the trash, then reached around her to open the door. "After you."

"Men can faint as much as women can. There's no gender bias to losing consciousness."

"Sure, but guys don't faint." He made the word sound foul. "They black out or pass out."

"Oh, I'm so sorry to have insulted your masculinity."

Looping an arm around her shoulders, he pressed a kiss to her temple, then whispered in her ear. "Good, you can make it up to my masculinity later. On your knees with a little begging thrown in should do it."

She huffed, elbowing him in the ribs. "Maybe you'll be the one begging."

"Oh, even better." He all but purred the words and she burst out laughing as they stepped out of the building and into the spring sunshine.

The Vegas heat wrapped around her—an oppressive blanket that contrasted with the cool coastal breezes she was used to in Half Moon Bay. Everything was different here. Even she was different here, indulging in passions she usually denied. The dry air filled her lungs, and she shook her head. She had no idea if this departure from the norm was a good idea or not, but she had committed herself to the week.

She wanted to see it through to the end.

CHaPTer
seven

U neasiness churned in the pit of Meg's stomach, and had since
Finn had suggested over lunch that she give up her room and
just stay with him. Who would know? The members of their group
were all on different floors and towers of the hotel. Sure, it made sense
and would cut costs, but even the thought of moving in with someone
for a week brought some ugly memories roaring back. Everything
about this affair seemed destined to make the past she'd ruthlessly
suppressed return to haunt her.

She'd refused his offer as politely as she could, and he'd let the topic
go, but she could tell he wasn't happy. Stepping into her room now,
she felt a disproportionate sense of relief that she had somewhere to
retreat. There was no need to be this glad about having her own space,
but she didn't have time to dwell. She had to change for the evening
out with the rest of their party—dinner and a show. Well, the women
and Finn were going to a show, the rest of the men were taking in a
heavyweight boxing match after dinner. *Yay, bloodshed.* Just what she

liked for dessert.

Stripping off the day dress she'd been wearing, she opened her closet for one of the two fancier dresses she'd brought with her. One was short, strapless and studded with silver sequins. Definitely the sexier of the two options. The other was fitted, knee-length navy-blue satin. Much more modest. She wavered for a few minutes before she grabbed the short and sexy one.

She slung it across the bed and headed into the bathroom to put on makeup, jewelry, and straighten her hair until it lay in a silky sheet down her back. It was more care than she'd taken on her appearance for her last three dates combined. She made a face at herself in the mirror.

Yeah, so maybe she wanted to look good for Finn. Even if this affair made her feel a little out of control, she still couldn't help but want him to find her attractive. Beautiful and irresistible would be nice, too. Not that he'd ever acted as if he found her anything but. However, the feminine side of her liked being wanted as much as any other woman.

After slipping on a pair of silver hoops, she tilted her head to make them catch the light and sparkle. Nice. Her phone rang and she flicked off the light switch in the bathroom before hurrying over to get the call. It was Karen.

She tapped the screen to answer. "Hi, hon. What's up?"

"Hello, Meg!" Karen's words lilted through the phone. "You're on speakerphone. I've got Anne and Julie here with me."

"The whole posse." Meg couldn't help the smile that formed on her lips. No matter how off-kilter she felt, her friends would always ground her. "How's everyone doing?"

A snort answered that. "Your dog ate Tate's shorts. He's offended."

Meg smothered a laugh. "Sorry about that. I'll replace them."

"Oh no. You don't need to do that. Tate can afford to buy new ones." Karen's voice shook with hilarity. "It was worth seeing the look on his face when he came out of the bedroom dangling his shredded boxers off one finger and looking at Hugo like he was the devil incarnate."

"Poor Hugo." He'd probably been even more mopey and depressive after someone had given him a nasty glare. The mutt was beyond sensitive.

"I love how none of us feel bad for Tate or his undies," Julie piped up.

"Pfft." Anne huffed. "Tate will be fine, but Hugo is always about half a second away from suicidal tendencies."

"So true." Meg wandered over to her suitcase, dug out the high heels she wanted to wear, and slipped them on. "Anne, how's Cami doing?"

"Cami's fine," said Anne. "I told her she needed to take a break for a couple of days. She's more upset about missing extra work hours over spring break than anything else."

"That sounds like her. She's such a little workaholic." The kid had been laser-focused even when she was in elementary school and Meg had babysat her. If she was worrying about getting work done, then she really was okay. It set Meg's mind at ease.

"Exactly," Julie interjected. "So, she's fine. Mrs. Kirby is still milking the drama, of course, but everything is basically back to normal."

Anne groaned. "Don't even get me started on the drama llama mama."

Laughter echoed through the phone, then Karen asked, "How's Vegas? Do anything buck wild? Get a tattoo? Pay for a lap dance? Buy a gigolo?"

"None of those options." Meg snorted. She picked up her dress and worked it over her head, pulling the phone away from her ear for a moment. "I'm not that wild."

Anne's voice turned coy. "Oh, come on. You have to have done something to pass the time."

"I went to a museum today. Did some shopping with you yesterday. Checked out the Bellagio fountains last night after you left." Then let the hottest man alive shag her brains out, but she kept that to herself. She wasn't ready or willing to talk about that, not even to her best friends, and Anne could only guess or assume what she might be up to this week. Unless Finn ratted her out—in which case, he had a slow and painful death ahead of him. "All right, girls, I have to go meet the drunk bunch for dinner. Then we're off to that Cirque du Soleil show, KÀ."

"Oh, that's so cool!" Julie exclaimed. "Let us know how it is."

"Please, I was going to get to see a heavyweight fight tonight, but now I'm missing it." Anne's words fell somewhere between plaintive and whining.

"You could always fly back," Karen suggested.

"Nah. I'd have already missed the match, it would be expensive to do two roundtrip flights, and someone has to stay here and make sure Cami doesn't sneak into work. God knows my mom would cave inside of thirty seconds." Anne huffed out an annoyed breath. "Megs, I hope you have a good time and that you manage to cut loose and do something crazy."

"I'm sure I'll have a great time." Meg resisted the urge to spill her guts about Finn. Maybe when it was over she'd be able to dish about this affair, but not now. "Night!"

"Bye, Meg!" Her friends echoed before they hung up.

The lies she told them ate at her. Lies of omission were just as bad as the boldface variety. You still always looked over your shoulder to wonder if anyone else was telling the truth behind your back. She hadn't told them everything about Brandon and Regina, and now she wasn't telling them about Finn. These women—these friends—had been with her for so long, and they knew everything else about her. They'd been with her when her parents broke up. They'd been with her when she'd sweated over SATs, college finals, grad school applications. They had specifics about every date she'd ever been on. They knew who'd been her first, her worst, who she'd loved and hated to lose. Everything. Except this.

Two secrets weren't so bad, but when you had the kind of friends who were always in your life and business, who told you the good and the bad and loved you no matter what you did, it was hard to hold back those details. Only guilt could do it. Guilt, shame, fear. It was too painful to divulge.

They would understand, but it would hurt them to know she hadn't trusted them. It would hurt her if any of them did the same to her.

She hated that.

The group had descended on the buffet at the Bellagio, which offered up five-star dining in an all-you-can-eat format. Pure evil, to Finn's way of thinking. He wandered around the various serving stations, loading his tray with far too many samples of amazing cuisine. Beef Wellington, fresh steamed lobster, chicken cordon bleu, filet mignon, roasted duck. And those were just for the main course. He had his eye on the dessert station, where he could see dishes of tiramisu, caramelized pears, cream puffs, bananas foster, and crème brûlée.

He couldn't decide what to go for first, and knew he was going to need to hit the hotel gym to work this meal off. Or go about fifty rounds on the mattress with Meg. He liked that option better, but figured the gym was still in his near future. His job demanded that he stay in shape if he wanted to keep up with rambunctious tweens, but he preferred exercising in the outdoors over slogging it out in a stuffy gym.

Winding his way back through the many tables and booths, he found his group, who seemed slightly more sober tonight. Though there *were* four open bottles of wine on the table, so he wasn't sure how long the sobriety would last. Ah, well. The more hazed with booze their memories were, the less likely they were to take note of anything he was doing with Meg.

He had to check the impulse to smile at her like an infatuated idiot as he sat down next to her. Seeing her with straight hair was a shock, but so was the tiny excuse for a dress she wore. It was damn hard not to reach out and stroke his hand over all that bare skin or run his fingers through her locks just to see how it would feel. But he managed to resist. Their colleagues would definitely notice right now, and he only had two rules he had to follow with her: discretion and deadline. He hoped to get rid of the second one, but the first one he agreed with. There was no reason to encourage uncomfortable questions and office gossip. He might not share her virulent horror of it, but he'd avoid it if he could.

So, he shifted his focus to Doreen, who sat across from him. "How was the strip club? Come out of there with any dollar bills left?"

"Not one." She grinned. "Thanks for asking."

"Lucky guys." He winked at her, making her giggle and flap a hand at him. The woman was twice his age, married with kids in college, so she loved when he flirted with her but wouldn't take it seriously.

Cindy leaned in from the end of the table. "There was one guy there... Meg, you should have seen him. We were taking bets on whether he'd had some kind of pec implants. No guy's chest could be that big without some help."

"And his jewels weren't shriveled enough for him to be on steroids." Karla propped her elbow next to her plate, finishing off a glass of red wine. "I've seen guys who juice and it's not pretty."

So had Finn, and he had to agree. Not that he spent much time staring at other men's junk, but he'd been in enough locker rooms after high school and college sporting events to have an idea of who was juicing and who wasn't. Some hid it better than others though.

Meg shrugged, forking a piece of fruit into her mouth. "Well, cosmetic surgery is on the rise for men."

Wait. They'd been serious about the implants comment? "They give men breast implants?"

The question was out of Finn's mouth before he could stop it. *Bad move, Walsh.* He was going to regret his incredulity, he could tell.

Four women turned to stare at him with varying degrees of hostility. Cindy crossed her arms. "What, women are the only ones who might have to get implants to improve their tips?"

Karla narrowed her eyes to dangerous slits. "Men shouldn't feel the same societal pressure that women do to be better looking?"

"Or to fight the aging process?" Doreen jutted a chin that had begun to soften and sag. The wounded look she gave him suggested the ills of society and men rested solely on his shoulders, and that he had a lot of explaining to do.

"Whoa." He put up his hands, trying to backpedal away from the obvious sore spot. "Look, I didn't mean that as a gender statement. If someone wants plastic surgery, they're more than welcome to get it, but they shouldn't feel pressured into it. I would never say something like that." Especially not in front of a group of opinionated women he respected and had to work with every day. He absolutely would not compound his stupidity by pointing out they'd gone to a strip club to objectify a bunch of greased-up men. That would only lead to more suffering and he wanted this topic dropped as soon as possible. "I'd just never heard of men getting breast implants before. I hear more about the ways people enhance performance, not appearance. That usually involves drugs instead of surgery."

Glancing at Meg for some moral support, he only saw her shake her head at him as if he were an idiot who'd brought this on himself. He nudged her leg under the table. Hard.

She rolled her eyes. "All right, ladies. He's been educated not to make a comment like that again. Leave him alone. Unless he does it again, in which case, feel free to sacrifice him on the altar of patriarchal misogyny."

"Thanks, I think." He grabbed the nearest bottle of wine and poured himself a large glass. After that grilling, he was definitely in need of fortification. He caught Frank's gaze at the other end of the long table and was offered a pitying glance. Finn toasted the other man with his wineglass.

A few seconds later, his cell phone vibrated in his pocket and he fished it out to find a message from Roger. *Are you sure you don't want to ditch the girls and come with us to the fight tonight? You can probably use Anne's ticket.*

Finn thought about it, really hard. The estrogen was a little thick over here and was starting to get toxic to the male of the species. Then Meg brushed against him as she reached for the saltshaker, the side of her breast sliding across his arm. Her scent teased his nose over the layers of food smells, and he knew there was no contest on where he'd rather spend the evening. With her. He only had a certain amount of time to work with and he needed to take advantage of it. He sent a message back to Roger confirming he'd be going to the Cirque du Soleil show with the girls tonight, but thanking him for the offer.

He took a swig of the wine, questioning his sanity, but knowing he wouldn't change his mind.

CHAPTER EIGHT

"This is so awesome!" Cindy bounced in the backseat of the cab, even though she was squished between the three other women. She leaned over the seat to look at Finn, her earlier hostility apparently forgotten. "Thanks for coming to the girl thing tonight, Finn."

"No problem. I wasn't up for the screaming crowds tonight." A flat-out lie. He liked a boxing match as much as the next guy, but this week was about spending time with Meg. That meant he'd have to watch the fight on DVR after he got home. He offered Cindy an easy smile. "I figure a Cirque show is probably a bit quieter."

"And prettier." She actually clapped in glee. "I went to 'O' the last time I was here, and it was so amazingly cool. I can't wait to see KÀ."

The cab pulled up to the curb of the MGM Grand, which spared him from coming up with a suitable reply. He stepped out and helped the women from the car, still not certain how they'd managed to sardine themselves into the back of the taxi. After checking with the concierge desk and getting directions to the theater, they wound their way through the casino. Finding their seats, he sat on the end of a row, Meg next to him, then Karla, Doreen, and Cindy.

Acrobats crawled out onto metal scaffolding mounted to the wall and ceiling, music blared, and the show started.

Unfortunately, it didn't take long for him to wish he'd gone with the guys to the fight. This was painful. Sure, he wanted to keep his eyes on the prize, and Meg was the prize, but he was bored out of his mind. It didn't help that he wasn't far from an exit. It took a serious exercise of self-control not to bolt.

The performance had no dialogue in any language he'd heard of. He was pretty sure it was gibberish. The acrobatics and sets were impressive, but the storyline wasn't really gelling for him. In fact, he wasn't sure there *was* a storyline—just people leaping and swinging around in bright costumes. If he had to think this deeply about whether there was a plot to follow, then it was definitely not his kind of entertainment.

He leaned down to whisper in Meg's ear. "Do you have any idea what's going on?"

Turning to whisper back, she replied, "I think those two are royalty of some kind and they're going to...um...no. No, I have no clue what's happening, but it's pretty to watch and these people are ripped. I bet that teeny princess chick could bench-press me."

He stifled a snort.

It was the boredom that made him do it. He glanced over and saw that all the women were absorbed by what was happening onstage. Dropping his hand to the seat beside his leg, he let his fingers inch over until he brushed against Meg's thigh. She stiffened, her gaze flicking to him and then to the other teachers.

"What are you doing?" She hissed the question in his ear.

"Shh," he admonished. "Watch the show."

Her head snapped around to face forward again. A subtle shudder ran through her when he edged his knuckles up her leg, bumping into the short hem of her dress. The silver scrap of fabric barely covered her thighs and he'd had to force himself not to stare at her when they'd been at dinner or he'd have had a permanent hard-on. At the moment, he was loving the cut of the garment. Less was definitely more. He eased a finger under the edge of it, hearing her breath catch.

Delicate little shivers began to run through her with every sweep of his fingers. Imagining how wet she was for him, how much she wanted him to take her, was far more engrossing than the Cirque du Soleil ever dreamed. Every moment seemed to stretch into one long, slow burn of anticipation. The flowery scent of her, the feel of her silky skin gliding under his fingertips. He did his best to keep his hand out of view of the other people in their party, but the forbidden aspect of touching her just sharpened the experience. He gritted his teeth to keep in a groan.

Teasing her meant teasing himself, and all he wanted right now was to bury himself in her tight, slick core until he was spent.

And then do it all over again.

Having her earlier at the Olympic exhibit wasn't enough. Last night hadn't been enough. He wasn't sure he'd ever get enough of her, and this week might lead to an addiction he couldn't quit. The idea was as tempting as it was terrifying. He'd had his share of women, probably more than his fair share, and he'd loved a few of them, but he'd never worried about what it might be like to live without them. He'd survived the breakups when they came, but...maybe that was why Meg drew him like a moth to a flame. He'd sensed all along she was the kind of woman who might rock the foundation of his world, if she stuck around long enough. He was fully aware that he could get in over his head in the next six days, crave her even more before the week was out, and be left high and dry.

It wasn't until now that he truly grasped how big a risk he had taken, how close to the edge of something life-changing he was, and how hard this fall might be. *Shattering* was a good word for it.

He shut down that line of negativity. If he went into this thinking he was going to lose, he'd kill any chance of winning. He was all-in this week, and there was no way he was backing off now.

Even if losing her in the end might be far worse than he'd ever imagined.

E very slide of his fingertips over her leg made tingles erupt across her skin. She could only pray that this show was over soon and she could drag him back to the hotel room for some fast, hot, dirty sex. Because that was what she needed right now. No-holds-barred shagging.

Her body was on fire, and only he could quench those flames for her. It took everything she had not to grab his hand and push it between her thighs where it could do the most good. She could have wept when the lights finally came on and all the performers took their bows. *Thank. God.*

She was on her feet and right on Finn's heels as he led the way out of the theater, the three musketeers following in their wake.

"That was even more awesome than I expected." Cindy was all but dancing around in a circle.

Meg slanted a glance at Finn, knowing he'd had even less of a clue than she did on what the show was actually about. The sets and costumes were gorgeous, but that was about all she could say for it. Maybe Vegas shows just weren't for her.

"I had a great time." He gave her a slow smile, and she could have kicked him. "Thanks for suggesting this, Cindy."

"No problem." The English teacher giggled. "I'm so glad you liked it too. What was your favorite part?"

He pretended to consider. "I think I liked the second half best. It really built to a climax."

Meg had to turn away for a moment or her face would totally give her away. Her cheeks must be beet red.

"Some of the acrobats were hot. Even hotter than the strippers last night. Totally ripped." Karla flipped her hair over her shoulder. "Watching them do all those stunts made me work up an appetite though. I have the munchies."

"Me too. I know we already had dinner, but I'm up for a snack." Doreen rooted around in her purse, pulled out her cell phone, and started tapping buttons. "Let me check what restaurants they have at this hotel."

Cindy eyed the casino like a kid in a candy store. The woman was enthused about everything. "I want to try the slots here and see if they like me better than at Caesars."

"I'm heading back to the hotel." Meg was not waiting around for them while she was all hot and bothered. It would be torment that reached truly inhumane levels. She gave Finn a pointed glance and he offered her a knowing grin in response, which sent another ripple of longing through her. She had it bad.

All three women goggled at her. Cindy asked, "Seriously? You're down and out already?"

"I'm not a night owl, ladies." Meg made an ugly face. "I look like this without my beauty sleep."

Peals of laughter met that statement. Doreen glanced up from her phone for a moment. "Lunch tomorrow?"

"Text me and we'll see if we can hook up." The phrase *hook up* did nothing to help slow down her raging libido.

"I'll make sure she gets back to the hotel safely." Finn leveled a stare at the other women. "You ladies stick together and watch out for each other, all right?"

"Yes, Mom," Doreen drawled with the kind of derision their students liked to dole out on a daily basis, but then she smiled. "Thanks for looking out for us. You're right. Wandering off alone at night in Sin City is probably not the best plan."

"My point exactly." He slid his hands into his pockets. "See you all in the morning?"

"Late morning, maybe." Karla snorted. "Try early afternoon. I might be out of bed by then. Maybe."

"Well, all right then. Don't have so much fun you get arrested." He mock leered at her and she sniggered.

"Night, all!" Meg wiggled her fingers in a wave, latched on to Finn's wrist with the other hand, and dragged him toward the main entrance of the hotel. The pathways through the casino looped around on themselves, which made navigating them a pain, but she was determined to get out of there as quickly as humanly possible. She was on a mission to get laid.

Her body throbbed with every step, her thighs sliding together, the shortness of her skirt letting air brush against skin that was usually covered. It made her more aware of her bare legs—legs that he'd stroked, teasing her beyond all reason. He set his palm against her low back as they walked, his fingers burning through her dress and increasing her agony. Her nipples tightened, jutting against her bodice. God, she wanted his hands on them, his mouth sucking at the sensitive peaks.

The cab line was thankfully short, and they soon slid into the backseat of a taxi. Finn sat close enough so that his thigh was plastered against hers. The quirk of his lips told her he crowded her on purpose.

She leaned forward, subtly slipping her hand into his lap, and addressed the driver. "Caesars Palace, please."

"Yes, ma'am."

Her fingers feathered up the length of Finn's shaft, and he made a strangled noise. She gave him an innocent "what's wrong" look and a muscle in his cheek began ticking. His shaft pulsed against her hand, the muscles in his thighs going rock hard as he tensed under her touch. His chest bellowed as his breathing sped. His eyes closed and his head fell back against the seat. She loved that she could make him tremble with need. The heady power of it ratcheted up her own cravings.

The stoplights were with them, and they sped down the Strip. Even then, it wasn't fast enough for her. She flicked her thumb over the head of his erection, making him jump. A low growl spilled out of him, and she shivered at the near-feral sound. Shooting him a sideways grin, she took her hand back as they pulled up to the hotel.

Finn threw a bill at the driver and manacled Meg's wrist with a steely grip. She barely managed to grab her purse before he hauled her out of the cab and across the lobby. She had to scurry in her heels to keep up with his long strides. Another couple got into the elevator with them, and she wasn't sure if she was grateful or resentful of their presence keeping Finn and her from going at it on the ride up. They reached Finn's floor and he pulled her out.

The moment the elevator closed behind them, she reached over and skimmed her hand over his backside. The man was built like a Greek god. It was a shame he had to wear clothes. Then again, the moment they were alone, she intended to rip every garment off his very fine body.

"I forget that you're not as sweet as you look." He shuddered when she squeezed his buttocks.

"You're welcome." She stood on tiptoe and nipped his earlobe as he fumbled with the key card for his room. "Hurry up, Walsh."

Snorting, he shook his head, but had the door open in moments. He held it open for her while he reached in and flipped on the light. She deliberately slid her body against his as she walked in. The choked sound he made was almost a groan, and it sent a thrill straight to her core.

She grabbed the front of his shirt, yanked him inside the room, and slammed the door shut. "Finally."

He opened his mouth to say something, but she was not interested in talking right now. His theater seduction had been far too effective. Shoving him against the wall next to the door, she had a second to watch his blue eyes widen in surprise before she kissed him. She bit his lower lip then pushed her tongue into his mouth. Her hands jerked at his shirt, wanting it off him, and she felt a few buttons rip in the process. This level of aggression wasn't like her, but she was too far gone to care right now. Her usual control and caution had evaporated like so much steam on a scorching hot day. It was exhilarating—freeing.

Then her hands were on his bare skin, satin over steel. She circled her thumbs on his nipples, loving the rush that hit her when he shuddered and moaned under her touch. He found the zipper on the side of her dress and yanked it down. The feel of his fingertips skating over her ribs sent tingles rippling across her skin. Her nipples peaked tighter, so she tweaked one of his.

He broke the kiss just long enough to pull her dress over her head and toss it aside. "Jesus, Meg. You are so amazing. I love this."

The word *love* coming from his mouth sent a pang through her, but he distracted her when he slid into her panties and filled his palms with her backside, squeezing, and she moaned in response. Her body arched into him, instinct overruling any rational thought her mind could generate. Though at the moment, it wasn't generating much.

"Strip," she ordered. "I want you naked."

"You too." His breathing was harsh rasps of air, his eyes glittering with diamond-hard lust. His hands went to his fly and he stepped out of his shoes as he shoved his pants and underwear down in one smooth motion.

Reaching back, she unhooked her bra and let it slide down her arms. Kicking aside her heels, she shimmied out of her panties and let them drop to the floor while she drank in the sight of Finn. All tanned skin, rippling muscles, and a hunger he didn't bother to hide. His gaze slid over her body, burning with incandescent lust. That he wanted her so much made her feel...lush, desirable, beautiful. It wasn't something she was used to, wasn't something she'd even have time to get used to, but she couldn't deny she liked it.

"Come here." She crooked her finger at him, and that was all he seemed to need.

His arm snaked around her waist, drawing her flush against him, and her nerve endings rioted at the full body contact. The crisp hair on his chest abraded her nipples, the rough silk of his skin making her shiver with pure, unadulterated need. Moisture pulsed in her core, her sex clenching on emptiness she desperately wanted filled. He pulled her off her feet and she wrapped her legs around his waist. His erection was heavy between her thighs. Close, but not close enough to where she wanted him.

Three strides took them across the room. He turned and fell back against the mattress, taking her with him. She landed on his chest, and straddled his waist as she pushed herself upright. Wriggling down his body, she felt his chest hair rasp against her sensitized breasts.

"Condom," he grated out.

Oh. She'd completely forgotten about protection. Something else that was unlike her. "Where?"

"In the nightstand." He pointed. "Didn't want to freak out the maids by leaving party favors lying around. Though I'd bet they've seen worse."

"No doubt." She knelt on the side of the bed, bending to reach for the nightstand drawer. The box inside was open with only a few missing. The ones he'd carried in his wallet, she realized. Somehow it was a relief that he wasn't halfway through the massive number of rubbers. She didn't want to keep him, but she didn't like the idea of sharing him with other women either. Shaking her head at *that* stupidity, she ripped one foil packet open and rolled the condom onto his rigid erection.

Swinging her leg over him, she resumed her earlier position, which spread her wide. Her heart raced with excitement. His thick shaft prodded at her opening. His hands clamped on her hips, but he didn't stop her from arching her torso and shoving her hips back to take him in one quick thrust. They both groaned at the sensation.

"Oooh." The shivery little sound escaped her throat. Letting her head fall back, she took a moment to relish the feeling of erotic fullness. He stretched her inner walls, and it was beyond amazing.

Planting her hands on his chest, she held his gaze as she lifted and lowered herself on him. She moved slowly at first, wanting to hold on to these moments. The heat that scorched through her, the wanton cravings, the way her body fit with his. Perfect. Too perfect to last.

"Ride me hard," he growled, his fingers biting into her thighs.

"Or else what?" Rolling her hips in a deliberately unhurried motion, she lifted her eyebrows. She was bluffing. Urgency hammered through her, and she dug her nails into his chest to cling to a slender tether on her control.

His full lips quirked, his eyes sparkling with a hint of laughter. "Would it help if I said please?"

"I don't know. Teasing me in the theater deserves a little punishment, don't you think?" She clenched her channel around him and watched a muscle jump in his jaw.

"Jesus, I want to come. I want you so damn much, Meg." He arched under her, shoving himself so deep it made her moan. It was almost too intense. "I can't get enough."

Neither could she. She wasn't even sure she wanted to. The thought shook her, so she swallowed and gave him what he'd asked for, distracting herself from the disturbing revelation. Bucking her hips, she took all of him, her sensitive flesh stimulated by the coarse hair at his groin. She could feel the hammering of his heart under her palms, the way his lungs heaved for air as they worked themselves faster and faster.

Sweat slid in beads down her skin, making her shiver as the cool air hit her hot flesh. His hands glided up her back, one slipped around to cup her breast and tease the tip. The other hand curled over her shoulder, pulling her tighter against the base of his shaft with each downward thrust of her hips. Moans spilled from her, and heat gathered deep within her. Soon, she would go over that wicked edge.

They raced each other for orgasm, and with each plunge, she could feel the tremors building in her sex. More. Now. She couldn't move swiftly enough to satisfy herself. Finn dropped his hand to the place their bodies joined, pressed in to stroke his finger over her nub. The effect was electric. She imploded, crying out as the first wave hit her. Contractions shivered through her sex, and she clenched around him. Riding him hard, she pushed her orgasm further, kept the pleasure going as long as possible. She watched his brilliant eyes lose focus as he hit climax, as well. His big body bowed in a hard arc between her thighs, lifting her knees off the mattress. She clutched his shoulders for balance, and he shuddered beneath her.

"Meg." He breathed her name with the reverence of a prayer. She collapsed onto his chest, and he caught her close, his arms wrapping tight around her.

When she began to resurface, disquiet wound through her. The total lack of control tonight was...terrifying. He shouldn't be able to reduce her to a quivering mass of need. She liked him too much and he turned her inside out. This wasn't good. Maybe it was time to draw back just a little. She didn't want to end things yet, but some breathing room might be best for both of them.

CHAPTER NINE

D amn, it was hot in Vegas. Even on a spring morning like this, it could turn blistering. Summer could sear the eyeballs. Finn wished he'd gone for a run on one of the hotel's treadmills instead of heading away from the Strip. It had been chilly when he'd started an hour ago, but the frigid desert dawn had burned away to scorching heat. Why his father had decided this was the place to retire, he'd never quite figured out. The desert was fine for visits, but living here full time? No way. The hellish temperature was not something he wanted to face constantly. Give him the mild coastal climate in Half Moon Bay any day.

Sweat poured down Finn's face, and his muscles ached from the punishing workout. He'd pushed himself hard on the run, trying to ignore his annoyance that Meg had decided not to spend the whole night with him after their wild lovemaking, reminding him that she had her own room and she should use it. Offering to share his had been a strategic error, he now saw. It had rattled her, though he wasn't entirely sure why. Too much intimacy perhaps, but he'd made the suggestion because his Meg was usually so logical. Paying for two rooms and only using one wasn't sensible.

So she was making sure she used her room instead of his. Damn it. Which gave them less time together than he'd expected when they first agreed to this arrangement. It was two steps forward and six steps back with her.

Frustration boiled within him, and he kicked his speed into a sprint, knowing he couldn't outrun himself. His lungs burned from the exertion and dry desert air, but he didn't stop running until he entered the hotel. Standing just inside the door, he bent and braced his hands against his knees, sucking in oxygen as the overly air-conditioned lobby made the sweat turn cold and clammy on his skin.

Straightening, he shoved a hand through his damp hair and strode through the ground floor of Caesars Palace. Halfway to the elevator, he switched directions, heading for the pool. He was still too keyed up to face his empty room and be reminded that Meg hadn't even texted him this morning. His running shorts would do just fine for a few laps in the water.

A huge bank of windows overlooked a series of pools. He followed the glass wall to the double doors that let him access the crystal-blue water.

He grabbed one of the towels for hotel guests and then found an unoccupied lounger. He dropped the towel, removed his shirt, and took off his sneakers and socks. A quick dive and he was engulfed in the cool liquid. Scissoring his legs, he made it halfway across the pool before he resurfaced for air. It felt good, stripping away the sweat and heat from his run.

After a few minutes he leaned against the side and propped his elbows on the ledge behind him. Children squealed and laughed, splashing each other. People sat in groups in chairs and on loungers, some talking, others waiting for food from the concession stand, and more than one lying out to tan.

A familiar, whooping laugh sounded to his left and he turned his head to look for Karla. *There*. On a lounger next to the pool. And right beside her sat Meg.

In a navy-blue bikini.

The sight was enough to send every ounce of blood in his brain rushing south. It didn't matter that he'd seen her naked before. Nope, those little scraps of blue fabric molding to her breasts and hips, contrasting with her creamy skin, just made him want to strip her. Slowly. The fact that she was reading a book while looking that flat-out sexy was an intense turn-on. Her curly hair had been tamed into two girlish braids, which somehow managed to be seductive.

They hadn't noticed him yet, thankfully, so he took a few minutes to look his fill and then got himself under control. The last thing he needed to do was show up, drooling over Meg and sporting a boner. He had a little more self-respect than that, no matter how much he might want her. Pushing away from the side, he paddled across the pool, dodged the playing children, and approached the two women.

"Morning."

"Hey!" Karla's smile was huge and welcoming, and for the first time since they'd landed in Vegas, she didn't have a drink in her hand. He'd half-expected a Bloody Mary or mimosa.

"Hi, Finn." Meg set aside her book and crossed her arms self-consciously over her breasts, even though her bathing suit was pretty modest compared to most of the women at the pool. He had to marvel again that a woman who was so reserved in public could be so uninhibited in bed. It was too bad that he loved the juxtaposition, found it insanely attractive.

He turned his gaze on Karla. "I take it you all got back okay last night?"

"Yeah, though we did have to call security on this drunk dude who wouldn't take Cindy's hell no for an answer. After that, we decided hanging out at our own hotel was more fun. So it wasn't as late a night as we thought it would be."

He frowned. "Is Cindy okay?"

Meg nodded, the braids on either side of her head bobbing with her movements. "She was just here. It was more obnoxious overeager guy who can't take a hint than creepy rapist guy who wants to get too handsy."

Shaking his head at the crap women had to deal with that didn't even occur to men, he was glad nothing worse had happened, and pissed Cindy had to put up with that in the first place. Either a woman was interested or she wasn't. End of story. Too bad he knew his fair share of guys who couldn't tell the difference or didn't really care that there was one. "I'm happy she's all right, and that you guys stayed together so she didn't have to deal with him alone."

"Yep." Karla stood and wrapped some silky bit of fabric around her. "I'm going to go find something to eat. You guys want to come along?"

Finn shook his head. "No, I just got back from a jog, so I really need to shower first."

Meg's gaze flicked uncertainly between Karla and Finn, and she bit her lip. "I want to read a little more, then go up to my room and change."

"All right. Later, guys!" Tipping her hand in a wave, Karla sashayed across the pool deck. More than one man stopped what he was doing to stare as she walked by.

"Karla is something else," Finn mused.

"She's a riot at staff meetings, that's for sure." Meg picked her book up, thumbing through until she found the right page. "Especially when she gets on Anne's nerves and they start competing for alpha female status."

He chuckled at the incredibly accurate description. But his mirth died as he watched her bury herself in her book. "What are you reading?"

"Hmm?" She hummed absentmindedly, not looking up. "Oh, a biography of Cleopatra."

"Why are you avoiding me?" He kept his tone quiet, but underlying it was...anger, hurt. It wasn't a good combination.

Her gray eyes lifted, wariness in their depths. "I'm not."

"What do you call this?" He tipped his chin toward the thick volume in her hand. "And what do you call last night, if not avoidance?"

Her throat worked for a moment, her mouth opening, then closing.

If he'd thought his frustration had been high on his run, it was nothing compared to this. He felt a muscle begin twitching in his cheek, and he clenched his jaw to hold back angry words that would only push her further out of reach. The best thing to do would be to get the hell away from her, let his temper cool off, and regroup.

Pulling himself out of the pool, he felt the water sluice off his body as he gained the deck. Meg's gaze widened, sliding over him, and naked want flashed in those stormy eyes. It just pissed him off even more. He bent forward, lowering his voice so no one would overhear. "Our deal was that we spent time together outside of bed."

"We have." Her chin set mutinously.

"I don't enjoy being treated like some cheap gigolo that you can screw and then discard. That's how last night felt." He hated to say it, but being strangled alive by the ugly emotions roiling inside him wasn't something he was willing to do. "If that's how you want it, I'm going to have to bow out of our...arrangement...because that won't work for me."

Her eyes widened—guilt, fear, and frustration that matched his own warring in her expression. "Finn..."

When she didn't continue, he shook his head. "If you're scared that you're going to like me a little too much by the time the week's out, and maybe even give in and date me when we get home, then be grown up enough to deal with it. Don't take it out on me. I don't deserve to be treated like crap."

"I know." Her gaze dropped and her tongue darted out to lick her lips. "I'm sorry."

"Just decide if you want to keep this thing going and let me know." He shoved both hands through his wet hair, sleeking it to his scalp. "You know where to find me."

Turning on a heel to stride over to his stuff, he toweled off roughly, then gathered everything into his arms and left. He didn't bother to look back. He frankly didn't want to know if she'd gone back to reading and ignoring him.

He showered quickly when he got to his room. After he was done, he stuffed himself into a pair of baggy board shorts and a T-shirt. What the hell was he going to do with the rest of his day? He'd planned on hanging out with Meg, but that wasn't high on his list now. Normally, he'd go visit his dad, but this weirdness with the new girlfriend made him reject that idea.

His cell beeped with a text, and he picked it up. It was from Meg. His gut churned a bit at having to deal with her again so soon. He was still pissed. Tapping an icon on the screen, he brought up the message.

Meet me in the lobby in 15 minutes?

His mouth tightened, and he shot a quick text back. *Why?*

There was a pause, and then her response popped up. *For some off-Strip fun, and so I can apologize again. Please?*

Sighing, he had to think hard before he decided what to do. For the first time since he'd met her, he didn't really want to be around her, but holding a grudge wasn't his style. He'd be cutting his nose to spite his face if he did it now. He replied with an affirmative and then went to dig a pair of sandals out of the closet.

He found her in the lobby standing near the white stone statue of three women in togas that dominated the middle of the space. He paused for a moment to watch her. She fidgeted, checked her watch, played with the strap of her purse. Checked her watch again. Her gaze met his when he started forward, and he could see the hesitation on her face.

"Hi," she said, her voice quavering a little. "I..."

"You?" he prompted, not giving an inch.

She blew out a breath. "I really am sorry, Finn. I shouldn't have ditched you last night. That was awful of me."

"Yeah, it really was."

Tears brightened her eyes, but she blinked them back. "I want to see this week through, if you're still interested. And I would understand if you don't want to. But you should know it's important to me to keep my own room. It is stupid, I realize that, but maybe some of the nights you could share my room with me instead of me always coming to you. Though, the bed is smaller because there were two doubles for when Anne was here."

It was a compromise, a peace offering, and as much as he'd like to demand all or nothing, he knew it would be foolish. He'd be left with nothing. As exasperating as it was, he needed to remember this was a marathon, not a sprint. "I think I can handle that, but if you want sex, it comes with spending the whole night together, no matter whose room we're in."

Her two braids bounced when she nodded. "I accept that." The grip she had on her purse strap turned white-knuckled. "And you were right. I am scared. Of myself, not of you. You're wonderful. Too much so."

"You don't have to be scared with me."

"I can't date a coworker, Finn. I have a hard enough time depending on guys after watching my mom deal with my dad's infidelity." Her lips compressed. "My job is important to me. I don't want to dread teaching because I have to see an ex when I go into school. That probably played a role in what happened with the last couple who dated at our school. You can't have a clean break from someone who works with you every day. I saw that so plainly with them."

"My job is important to me too, but I don't go into a relationship with a woman assuming it will fail. I also know you can have an amicable breakup. Not all of them are like your parents' or those other teachers'. You have to know that." Crooking his finger under her chin, he made her meet his gaze. "There's something more to this coworker thing than just having watched that couple's relationship melt down."

He was taking a stab in the dark, going with a gut feeling.

Her eyes deepened to a stormy gray, but she nodded. "That couple...the woman accused the man of cheating on her. Like my dad did with my mom. It just made me see how those two situations could combine into my worst nightmare."

"Oh, damn, sweetheart." He cupped her cheeks between his palms, his heart aching for what she'd been through, wishing he could erase it for her. "I am so sorry. Not every man cheats. I don't cheat."

"I know that, logically." She wrinkled her nose. "But fear isn't logical. I just don't want to end up like my mom, and I don't want to end up with a bad relationship I can't escape. I'd have that if I dated a teacher and we broke up."

"We aren't your parents and we aren't those other teachers. Give me a chance to show you how unfounded your fears are with us." He pressed a finger to her lips to stop her from responding. "I don't want you to answer that now. Just be with me this week, that's all I ask. Don't run and hide from this."

He wanted her trust, all of it, but it was easy to see she wasn't ready for that. The quick, deep connection they shared was something he celebrated and she feared. He only hoped he had enough time to convince her he was right, but pushing too hard wouldn't get him anywhere, so he backed off the heavy emotional stuff. "You said you wanted some off-Strip fun. I know of a local history museum you might like. About atomic testing in Nevada."

She tipped her head toward the exit. "Sounds interesting, but we have other plans today."

"We do?"

"Yep." A genuine smile touched her lips and reached her eyes. She checked her watch. "Uh-oh, we're running a bit late."

Spontaneity wasn't exactly her forte, so he was more than a little curious. "Late for what?"

"The bus. Come on." She jogged outside and he had no choice but to follow or be left behind. They crossed one of the walking bridges and ended up in a small crowd waiting for public transportation. "Oh, good. This one's ours."

A two-story bus pulled up, and they joined the line shuffling forward to get on. "Where are we going?"

"It's a surprise. You'll see." She fished a few bills out of her pocket and bought them both day passes. Handing one to him, she led the way through the packed lower level and up to the second floor, which was far less congested. They found two seats together and grabbed them.

He laid an arm across the back of her chair, scanning her features for a moment. "I don't even get a hint?"

Looking excited and more than a little pleased with herself, she shook her head. "Nope. We're going where I say, and you just get to wonder."

"I do, huh?" He leaned over and kissed the side of her neck, just because he liked to make her react. "You're suddenly all bossy and take charge."

"Yep." She tipped her head, giving him as much access to her neck as he wanted. No shrinking away because they were in public. Good.

"That's kind of hot," he whispered in her ear, then nipped at the lobe.

"Shut up, Walsh." She bumped him with her shoulder, and he watched a blush creep up her neck, but he also saw her cheeks crease in a little grin.

He rested his head against hers and closed his eyes for a minute. The light scent of her perfume filled his nostrils. He had no idea what the hell he was doing anymore. There was no doubt he wanted her on every level. More with every second that passed, but the emotional roller coaster was faster and wilder than he'd ever imagined. He was going to do his best to hang on for the ride, but his confidence in how well this week-long gamble would pay off was dwindling. It was wrenchingly painful to realize how much he was coming to care for her—so much so that her not wanting to spend the night had been a knife to the chest. This could end in a serious disaster, and he wasn't sure he could do anything to stop it.

The only thing he was sure about was he didn't want to walk away.

The only thing she was sure about was she didn't want to walk away. Not now. Not yet. Meg wanted her week with him. It had been awful to have him confront her about her behavior, but she couldn't say she blamed him. She'd been terrible. Something else to add to her less-than-stellar history with men. But the truth was, Finn was right. She'd been scared and she ran from her fears. They were two days into this affair and already her resolve was wavering far too much. Where would her resolve be by day seven?

She didn't know and that scared her. But being nasty to Finn to save herself wasn't the answer. He didn't deserve that. Hell, he deserved far better than she could offer, and that was the sad truth. She wished it weren't, but there was nothing she could do to change it. Still, she'd agreed to the week, given herself permission to be a little reckless for seven whole days, and she was selfish enough to want all of them. Even if it was scary. Even if she had to give a little ground not to hurt Finn any more than she feared she was going to. The way he looked at her...she knew he liked her, knew he cared, and she both loved and hated knowing that. It wasn't just sex for him. It never had been, and treating him like a sex toy was a slap in the face to a good man.

She'd do better in the future.

The bus rocked around a corner, and being on the upper floor just exaggerated the ungainly sway of the massive vehicle. She pulled herself out of her morose thoughts and looked around to see what intersection they were at. Missing their stop would be a bad thing.

"Here we are." She bounced out of their seat, grabbed Finn's hand, and dragged him along behind her.

"We're in the middle of nowhere," he stated. "Where are you taking me?"

"You'll see. Come on."

They made it to the ground floor and just managed to catch the door before it closed. She hopped out onto the sidewalk, flinching a bit as the heat slammed into her full force.

"Okay. There's where we're going." She pointed to a nondescript building, and his gaze followed the direction of her finger.

The big sign over the building made his jaw drop. *Gold & Silver Pawn Shop.* "No way."

"Yes way."

"It's the shop from *Pawn Stars.*" A huge grin split his face.

Smugness filled her at the disbelief and pleasure on his face. He'd been so focused on doing whatever she wanted while they were here, she was glad she could offer him a little of that in return. It didn't make up for her being a complete jerk to him the night before, but it was a start.

She tried for a modest shrug. "You said you wanted to come here, so I did a bit of research."

He yanked her into his arms. Then he kissed her very thoroughly, bending her backward so she had to grab his shoulders to keep her balance. Heat exploded through her and it had nothing to do with the weather and everything to do with her unquenchable lust for Finn Walsh. His tongue slid between her lips and he feasted on her mouth. They didn't come back up for air until a loud wolf whistle pierced the air and she heard applause.

Looking around, she saw a couple of bikers mounted on Harleys parked next to the shop. Cracking up, she covered her face and burrowed into Finn's chest. Being turned on in public was more than a little awkward. From the corner of her eye, she saw him give the bikers a wave before he drew her into the pawn shop.

A few of the people from the television show were behind the counter, but Meg and Finn just wandered around looking at everything. He dragged her over to a display of baseball collectables, and she squealed, then clamped a hand over her mouth when people turned to stare at her.

"You're so cute when you blush." He ran his finger down her cheek and neck.

She pursed her lips. "There's nothing wrong with blushing. Or being cute. I think going with one's natural talents is a good thing."

"If it's not broken"—he swooped in and kissed her lightly—"don't fix it."

"Exactly." She fanned her face to cool her flushed cheeks.

His smile was easy, and gratitude expanded in her chest. She was so glad he wasn't staying mad at her, and she knew she shouldn't care what he thought of her, but she did. She pushed the thought away. She was tired of beating herself up over how she felt. This week was supposed to be fun. There would be plenty of time when she got home to overanalyze every little thing she'd done. So she let Finn take her hand and lead her toward a display with a medieval jousting helmet.

"I think you might like this, Meg."

She thought she might too, if she could let herself.

CHAPTER TEN

I t was going too well, and for some reason, that worried Finn.

He pushed himself to greater speed on the stationary bike he rode in the hotel gym while he considered. Meg hadn't tried to pull back since the night they'd gone to the Cirque du Soleil, though they now split their time between her room and his. But...it was too perfect. It fit just right, and he had no clue what he was going to do if she decided to end it after this week. They only had two days left, and he didn't know where they stood.

But he was falling for her. Hard.

It wasn't as if he hadn't seen it coming. He'd known the possibility was there when he'd gotten Anne to talk Meg into this trip. Sensing it was possible and having it become a reality were different things, and the reality was much more complicated than he'd imagined. He was hanging on to his sanity by a thread, trying not to let himself fall all the way. Loving her and losing her would be...catastrophic. The thought was gut-wrenching, and he shoved it out of his mind.

A cloud of dread hung over him, growing darker and heavier as the days slid by. Tomorrow, he had to deal with dinner at his dad's.

It would also be his last night with Meg before they left town.

"Hey, Walsh! Spot me, would you?"

The voice yanked him back to the here and now, and he turned to see Frank lying on a bench, ready to lift some free weights. Using his shirt to swipe the sweat from his face, Finn hopped off the stationary bike. The display said he'd gone nearly twenty miles, but he'd been so engrossed in his thoughts that he didn't remember much of it. He'd just pedaled.

He hadn't even seen Frank come in, and from the sweat rings on his shirt, the other man had been working out for a while. Finn stepped over to the bench and kept his hands on the bar while Frank began pumping the weights up and down. His face went red, and beads of sweat formed on his brow as the rep count got higher.

"Do you know where everyone else is today?" The words were a bit breathless as Frank spoke.

Finn watched the veins pop out on his colleague's forehead, wondering if he should warn him to take it easy. "The ladies are meeting for brunch right now at some kind of frilly tearoom, and I think we're all doing dinner at the Paris. A place called Mon Ami Gabi that has a patio looking over the Bellagio fountains. Then anyone who's interested is taking the ride up the fake Eiffel Tower."

Frank gasped, "Not your style, Walsh?"

"I'll go if everyone else does." Tightening his grip on the bar as Frank wobbled, Finn lifted the weights and set them back in place.

Flopping backwards, Frank wheezed for a few moments before speaking. "I'll give it a try. One more ride to go on."

Finn held out a hand to pull the other man to his feet. "Not as fast as some of the others on the Strip, though. How did you like the one at the New York?"

His eyes lighting up, Frank flapped an excited hand through the air.

"Fantastic! The engineering that goes into those rides is just amazing."

And this was why Frank was the math teacher and Finn handled P.E. This was just not his interest. They took turns sucking down some water from the drinking fountain, and Finn sighed when the cool liquid flowed over his parched tongue. He'd managed to forget his water bottle. Not a smart move, but it would have been worse if he'd been out in the Vegas heat without it.

"Want to grab some coffee?" Frank asked.

Caffeine sounded far too good, probably because Finn had been keeping Meg up most of the night, every night. If his time was limited, he couldn't waste it by sleeping, could he? That was what coffee was for. "A double espresso might be in order."

Chuckling, Frank led the way to the nearest caffeine dealer.

B runch had somehow turned into shopping, and Meg followed along behind Doreen and Cindy with her arms loaded down with bags. Karla walked beside her, burdened with even more bags. Meg had no idea how it was possible, but Doreen had found every deal the Strip had to offer. She'd dragged them into so many shops having sales they'd started to blur for Meg. They'd been to The Venetian, Planet Hollywood, and everywhere in between, and ended at the Forum Shops at Caesars Palace. She'd bought postcards to send to Anne's sisters, cheesy souvenirs for her friends, a Vegas snow globe for her mom, and a set of Vegas-themed trading cards for her dad.

When the other women weren't looking, she'd also purchased a slinky teddy to wear for Finn. If tomorrow was her last night with him, she wanted to make it memorable. She'd like to see those blue eyes of his pop open wide and lust that could curl her toes reflected on his handsome face. The sheer, sexy little number she'd picked up might make that happen, even though she turned bright red just knowing she'd bought the thing.

They trailed out of the Forum Shops and into the hotel proper, smothering their laughter at the sight of a mannequin in one of the windows. It was dressed in an outfit that could put Liberace to shame. On the way, they passed the hotel's food court and a massive theater complex.

"Hey, guys!"

Meg startled as Frank popped out from between two rows of slot machines. Finn was right behind him. The musky scent of male sweat wafted off them. Both wore baggy mesh basketball shorts and a tank top, but Finn's was pale pink.

Karla snickered. "I think someone dropped his white shirt in the laundry with something red."

"Ah, no." He turned around so they could read the back. There was the classic pink ribbon for breast cancer awareness along with the saying, *Save Second Base.*

Everyone chuckled as they read it. "Nice."

He faced the group again, waving a large coffee cup. "I do the walk for breast cancer every year in San Francisco in my mom's name. She died of it about five years ago."

Doreen made a sympathetic noise, Cindy reached out to pat his shoulder, and Karla said, "That's a really nice way to commemorate her."

Nodding, Meg forced herself to stay where she was and say nothing or she might be tempted to hug him. Cancer was such an awful way to lose someone. Poor Finn.

"It's something I like to do for her. She was an amazing mom." He took a final swig of his coffee and lobbed the cup into a nearby trash can.

Empathy squeezed inside her, and she ached for him. But it mingled with a growing anger on her own behalf. It had caught her by surprise at odd times the last few days and hit her again now. Because... God, could he get any more wonderful? It just wasn't fair that he had to be her coworker. Why couldn't he be a lawyer or dentist or electrician? Anything but a teacher at Half Moon Bay Middle School.

The injustice of it seared through her. She wished that something about their situation was different, that there was some way around that one blockade. But there wasn't or she would have found it by now. They suited each other so well on so many levels, and it was still doomed. How sucktastic was that? He might argue that it didn't matter that they were coworkers or remind her that they weren't her parents, but he hadn't seen what she'd seen or been through what she'd been through. If he had, he might not be so quick to dismiss her fears. And it still pissed her off that she shouldn't—*couldn't*—keep him.

He gestured down at his sweat-soaked clothes. "I think a shower is in order. I'll see all of you for dinner?"

"Mon Ami Gabi is one of my favorite restaurants in Vegas." Doreen's face creased in a smile. "My husband and I like to eat there when we come here. He's a bit miffed I'm cheating on him with my friends to go there."

"Aw, poor hubby. Too bad he couldn't come this week. Maybe you can get him a really great present to make up for it." Meg lifted her arms as high as she could, which wasn't far because they were loaded down with bags. "You do have an outstanding gift for shopping."

Covering her mouth, Doreen giggled. "I do, don't I?"

"Yes, and before I lose feeling in my hands, I'm going to take all this stuff to my room. Dinner at seven, right?"

"Right," Cindy replied. "I made reservations. Everyone just meet over there."

"See you at seven!" Meg gave a little wiggle of her fingers to wave goodbye, though her wrists were starting to throb from the heavy load of the plastic bags cutting into her skin.

Finn's gaze moved over her in a quick sweep before she turned away. It was subtle enough that she doubted anyone else picked up on it, but his expression told her he wanted her. Now, always. A frisson of heat passed through her. She could feel his gaze on her as she walked away, but she couldn't look back with everyone else watching. Damn it.

When it came to Finn, she could never really have everything she wanted. The thought depressed her.

F inn's phone rang the moment he stepped into his hotel room. Hoping it was Meg, he grabbed it, but the display showed Anne's name and number. He fought a groan, knowing better than to ignore a call from her. "Hello?"

"Hey there, lover boy." Her words had a teasing lilt. "How's everything going?"

He cringed at the term *lover boy*. "Fine."

"Just fine?" He could practically hear her eyebrows arching.

Injecting as much cheer into his voice as he could muster, he said, "Really, super fine."

She harrumphed. "I can fly back there and give her an excuse never to speak to you again."

Toeing out of his shoes, he tucked the phone between his shoulder and ear, then bent to tug off his socks. "Do it and I'll kill you. Seriously dead."

"Oh," she purred. "Then things are going better than even really, super fine. How soon after I left did you score?"

Yeah, like he was answering that question. But she wasn't going to be put off by evasions, so he kept it as short as possible. "We have an agreement for the week."

"An agreement." Her tone was doubtful.

"No strings attached." Tapping the button to turn on speaker-phone, he set his cell down and then shucked his shirt. When his own stink annoyed him, it was definitely time to shower.

A crack of gleeful laughter sounded through the phone. "Good for her. I wasn't sure she had it in her."

"She does." A rueful smile touched his lips. "It was her idea, not mine. I wanted a date, she wanted a lot less."

"Or more, depending on how you look at it."

"It's less, trust me."

There was a long pause. "Are you going to be okay with this?"

"I'm...not sure." He rubbed the back of his neck. "I like her, Anne. This week has made it more than just like. But she's determined that it's a spring fling only, and...I'm not sure I'm going to be able to change her mind anymore." He was less and less certain by the minute. Doubt was starting to weigh down on him and what had once felt like a game wasn't fun anymore. There was far too much riding on the outcome when they were playing for keeps.

Somehow watching her walk away with her shopping bags had hit him, and he realized he was forty-eight hours away from watching her walk away for good. Jesus, it sucked.

She snorted. "You went into it pretty cocky, and she's taken you down a few pegs."

"Confident, not cocky," he protested. "I didn't assume anything, I was just hoping like hell I could pull it off. That hope is fading."

At this point, it was almost dead. She'd shown no real signs of backing off her one-week-only stance, and he was a hairsbreadth away from falling in love with her. Helpless desperation gripped his gut.

"She's a stubborn girl, our Meg."

"And we like her that way." He liked everything about her. He even liked how graciously she'd apologized when she'd messed up. It said good things about what a real relationship would be like with her, where confrontation and compromise were inevitable.

"Yes, we do." Anne sighed. "Don't give up, okay? That big blowup we had between two teachers a few years back, the ones who were together?"

"Yeah, I've heard of it." More than he ever wanted to.

The line rustled as if she'd shifted the phone. "It hit Meg really hard—harder than anyone else in the school district. She was pretty tight with the guy, Brandon, and the fact that he had to leave HMB to get away from the whole mess really got to her. I think being so close to it made it that much worse. It reminded her a lot of her parents' breakup, which redefined ugly, public, and scandalous."

"I just...we're not those people, we weren't involved, and we don't have to end up like that." He pressed his fingers into his eyes, a familiar frustration welling in him. He felt like a broken record, but as true as it was it didn't seem to make a damn bit of difference.

"I know, but...don't give up, okay? She's just scared. I can understand why, but don't let her fear get in your way. She deserves a guy who would fight for her, even if it means fighting her fears. I'm hoping you can be that guy, or I wouldn't have left her there with you."

A small smile lifted his lips. "That was pretty profound, Anne."

"Yeah, well." He could all but hear her shrug. "My friends should have the best."

"Thanks." He was...touched...that she thought he would be the best thing for Meg. Anne wasn't an easy woman to impress, especially when it came to anything involving her friends. Meg had a similar loyalty to her little group. He had to wonder what the other two friends were like. He'd never met them.

"Good luck." A muffled shout sounded from the background. "Oh, crap. Mom and Cami are going at it again. Keeping Cami cooped up in the house is not going well. Gotta run!" She hung up before he had a chance to say goodbye.

He removed his shorts and underwear, leaving them in the middle of the floor while he headed for the bathroom. The rush of hot water over his skin felt good, but did little to wash away all of the worries that pressed down on him.

A soft knock sounded on the bathroom door. "Finn?"

Meg. She'd finally used the spare key card he'd given her for his room. He called out, "I don't need housekeeping today."

"That's too bad," Meg replied, mirth in her tone. "Maybe there are other services I can provide instead."

"Come on in and show me what you've got to offer." He tilted his head to listen for her movements, but there was a silence for several long moments.

The shower curtain slid back and Meg hopped in naked, her hair tied up in a loose knot on her head. She gave him a siren's smile as she stepped in behind him. His shaft began to harden in response to her nearness. She got to him, and the effect didn't seem to be diminishing. It was intensifying.

Her arms wrapped around him from behind, her breasts pressed against his back. He closed his eyes, the feel of her so damn sweet. One of her hands slipped up to tease his nipple, and he shuddered as it tightened for her. When her other hand coasted down his abs, tracing the muscles before closing around his shaft, he groaned.

"Are these services you're interested in?" Her lips brushed his shoulder blade.

"God, yes." He set his hands against the shower wall, letting her play with him as she pleased. Water sluiced down him and amplified every single sensation. "Don't ever stop."

The words were ripped straight from his soul. *Don't stop touching him, being with him, being his.* She paused in her ministrations, as if sensing his words had more weight than they should, but then she kissed his back and twisted his nipple. The breath whooshed out of his lungs as lust and pain and rejection mingled. He swallowed and pushed aside everything but the physical. That was what she wanted, and at the moment, it hurt too much to give more than that.

Her grip tightened on his shaft, stroking him until his teeth clenched and fire roared through his veins. The water slipped in a caress over his skin, the heated steam wrapping around him like an embrace. He drove his hips forward, moving with her stroking fingers. Meg bit his shoulder, and he jolted, his erection swelling even more. Her low laughter echoed in the bathroom. "I put a condom on the ledge of the tub before I got in. Care to use it?"

"Yes," he groaned.

Turning, he enjoyed the view of her bending over to fetch the rubber. He wasn't usually an ass man, but hers was exceptional. He curved his hand over one cheek, squeezing. Then he dipped down to bite the other one.

"Finn!" Squealing, she jerked upright, the condom clutched in her fingers.

He grinned, snagging the protection from her and putting it on in seconds. "Come here."

She stepped close, pressing herself against him, and the water glued their bodies together. "I want you."

"For now." The words hit him hard and he saw her gaze darken.

Slamming his mouth down over hers, he put enough force behind the kiss to be punishing. Instead of pulling back, she slipped her arms around his neck and arched into him. Her tongue dueled with his, and she lifted one leg to twine around his hip, opening herself to him.

The kiss was all lips and teeth and tongue as their need spiked. He slid his hands over her soft curves, filling his palms with her butt. Backing her against the shower wall, he pulled her up so she could cinch her legs around his waist. *God, yes.* He plunged into her, going deep on the first thrust. Her nails scored his shoulders, and she moaned.

His heart raced, the sound of his blood rushing in his ears. His lungs heaved as he struggled to draw in air fast enough, still he didn't release her mouth. The squeeze of her slick sex on his shaft was fantastic, the friction mind-blowing as their bodies moved under the hot spray. His muscles burned as he pistoned in and out of her, faster, harder, wanting to forge them into one, wanting to make sure she knew she was his whether she liked it or not. The roughness of his possession was unlike him, but she pushed him beyond all semblance of control. He took her hard and fast and he absolutely loved it. She whimpered into his mouth, her core fisting on him with every hard shove into her sex. She was close. He could sense it, feel it. The last few days had given him the ability to read her body.

Rolling his hips, he ground himself against her. Her thighs clamped on his waist, and she threw back her head, crying out as orgasm shook through her. "Finn!"

A groan was his only response and he slammed into her, driving toward his own release. One, two, three more thrusts and he was shuddering against her, come jetting from him.

He let his forehead drop to her shoulder as he sucked in oxygen. Her hand stroked through his wet hair, and he liked it too much. He liked her too much for his own good. All he could do now was pray. He hadn't been this desperate for some kind of miracle since his mom got sick. God help him if this ended as badly as that had.

CHAPTER ELEVEN

"D ad offered to pick us up, but I wasn't sure if that was going to mean twenty minutes of awkward silence with his girlfriend or what, so I just said we'd take a cab." Finn rambled, repeating something he'd already said. Twice. He sounded nervous, so Meg slid her hand into his and squeezed. He closed his eyes and tightened his fingers around hers. "We're almost there."

"It's going to be okay," she soothed. "Even if it's really bad, I'm here and I'll do what I can to deflect the badness."

They turned into what looked like a sprawling condo community. The cab took them past a pool and a rec center. The pool had an aqua aerobics class going on and a few seniors with yoga mats were walking into the rec building.

She craned her head to look around. "It's busy around here."

"Yeah." He swallowed, his thumb rubbing over her palm. "I think my dad likes that about the place. He said it didn't feel like a convalescent home where people went to die."

"Good call."

Nodding, he braced when they went over a speed bump. "He toured a few places before he picked this one. I liked that they had medical staff on call at all times. My dad's in amazingly good health, but you never know. What if he falls and breaks a hip or develops a condition that requires extra care?"

The taxi pulled to a stop, and Meg waited while Finn paid the driver. She glanced around, but the buildings all looked the same. Tidy, newly painted, but with the blandness of any planned community. "I can see how that would take a load off your mind. My parents are still a few years off from a retirement community, but I'm making a mental note for when they do start looking at them."

Finn took her hand to steer her toward one of the staircases. "My parents were in their late thirties when they married and had me, so they were always older than most of my friends' parents."

"Mine were pretty young when they had me. Still in their teens." Which might have contributed to some of the problems they'd had later. They'd been too young, too immature. Especially her dad. He hadn't known what he wanted out of life, and when he'd tried to experiment and figure himself out, his marriage had imploded. Not that she was making an excuse for him—she had always painted him as a pure villain in the situation, without thinking about what might have caused it. Her parents had fought a lot before he'd strayed. He should have ended things before he found a new bedmate, but that spoke to a lack of maturity too.

Funny that she'd never thought of it that way. She'd always just seen how it affected her and how not to go through that again. Selfish, perhaps, but she'd been a teen when they broke up. Teens were self-absorbed.

Finn drew her over to a door with a massive fish emblazoned on the welcome mat. She pursed her lips to stop a grin from forming. "I can guess what your dad's hobby is."

"Yep. We take a backpacking and fishing trip at least once a year. He also likes baseball, for the record." He let a breath ease out, then turned and caught her face in his hands. "Thank you for being here tonight. Even if this could be a suckfest."

"I'm glad I'm here for you." And she meant it. Even if she couldn't be with him in the long run, she could do this for him. Everything this week had unraveled for her. She felt like she was coming apart at the seams. What she knew was wrong felt so right, and what she shouldn't want, she craved. Her orderly world wasn't as safe as she'd thought it was—the future wasn't as clear as it had once been, and that was dangerous. But she could be here for Finn now, and worry about the future later.

He dropped a quick kiss on her lips. "All right. Let's do this."

The door opened before he could knock, and Meg came face-to-face with what Finn would look like in forty years. Except for the brown eyes, the similarity was uncanny. It was a bit eerie to see the two men together, especially when Finn's dad dragged him in for a hug and then they stood right next to each other facing her.

"Dad, this is Meg Phillips."

He could have qualified it and said they were friends or they worked together, but he didn't. Because none of those things were the truth—not the whole truth anyway.

She smiled and held out her hand. "It's nice to meet you, Mr. Walsh."

"Call me John." His grin was wide, welcoming, and a little bit speculative as he glanced from her to Finn and back again. He engulfed her hand with his, giving a firm shake. "Come on in."

The condo was larger than she expected. There was a wide living room, what looked like an office opening off one side, a kitchen and a long hall with enough doors to indicate several bedrooms. The decorations were worn, and she assumed they were from the house he and his late wife had shared. There was definitely a feminine touch.

"Can I get you something to drink? Water, juice, wine, beer? I might even have the fixings for a margarita, if you feel like a cocktail."

Over John's shoulder, she saw a woman step out of the kitchen. She was short and round with cropped salt-and-pepper hair and a ready smile. She also wore eye shadow in a shade of electric turquoise not found in nature, a bright purple caftan, and at least a pound of jewelry hung around her neck. There was a large, sparkly ring on every finger that flashed when she waved. "Hi, I'm Ursula."

Well, this should be interesting.

F inn was relieved that the woman didn't look a thing like his mother, but the eye-searing shades she was sporting made him do a double take. That was one hell of a fashion statement.

Ursula came toward them and thrust her hand out for him to shake. "It's good to meet you, Finn. Your father talks a lot about you."

He couldn't say the same for her, but he kept that to himself. This whole experience was surreal. He took her hand. "Nice to meet you too, Ursula."

"I doubt that," she said bluntly, softening it with a smile. "But maybe it will be after you get to know me."

The honesty was refreshing, and he had to chuckle. "I hope you're right."

"I'm sure of it. I'm very likeable." Her dark eyes twinkled, and she pivoted toward Meg before he could respond to her statement. "Is it

Meg or Megan? I couldn't quite hear from the kitchen."

"Just Meg, thanks." Meg's eyebrows arched as she took in the color-ful appearance of the older woman, which only got more flamboyant when Ursula was close enough to see that every stone in her rings was a different color and from her necklaces hung a crucifix, a Star of David, a pentacle, and a portly little Buddha. Meg met his gaze, and he saw merriment shining in her gray eyes.

Just like that, he relaxed. This might be strange, but it would be all right. Meg was here, his dad seemed to be the fishing nut he'd always been, the condo looked the same, and Ursula was an exotic bird that Finn had no doubt would be entertaining.

Letting out a breath, he smiled for the first time since they'd left the hotel. "I'll take a beer, if you've got one. Meg...you probably want a glass of water?"

"Yes, please."

Dinner was less uncomfortable than he'd thought it would be. It helped that his dad and Ursula didn't do any public displays of affection. She occasionally put her hand on his shoulder or arm, but that was it. Finn appreciated that they were letting him ease into them being touchy-feely. Ursula was a riot. There was no other word to describe her. She was born in Kansas, but in her twenties had left home and joined a commune, decided she didn't like commune life and floated like a vagabond around the world until she ended up in Vegas. She'd met his father on a trip the retirement home had organized several months before. They didn't specify when meeting had turned into dating and Finn didn't ask.

It also helped that Meg sat next to him during dinner and had her leg pressed against his under the table. For some unnamable reason, the physical contact kept him grounded. He didn't miss the way Ur-sula and his dad looked at Meg and him. The older couple seemed to be hoping for some kind of explanation of Finn and Meg's relationship. But Finn wouldn't have known where to start, so he kept silent on the subject, and Meg did too. Instead, Meg took the focus off Finn and regaled them with hilarious stories of her three best friends, babysitting Anne's quirky sisters, dealing with some of her own wacky and wild students, and competed with his dad on baseball trivia.

"Okay, I'm just going to ask," Ursula started, but his dad's hand came down on her arm, squeezing her into silence.

"We're just colleagues. Really. *Just* colleagues." Meg's smile was too bright to be real. "Where's the restroom?"

Dad pointed her in the right direction, while Finn stood and began gathering the dinner dishes. Didn't it just figure that the most awkward moment in the evening would come from *his* love life rather than his father's? Finn didn't know whether to laugh or put his fist through a wall. He did neither, just took the plates into the kitchen, set them down and braced his hands against the counter, blowing out a breath. "Christ."

"It's hard, loving a woman." His dad came up behind him, setting a hand on Finn's shoulder.

"I don't—"

"Don't you?" The question was quiet, but it shut Finn down.

Yes, he did love her. Jesus. He'd been holding back, telling himself not to go over that cliff, but it was too late. The truth slammed into him with all the power of a sledgehammer to the chest. He was in love, and she still insisted they were *just* coworkers. What a nightmare.

"I like your Meg. I hope things work out with you."

His laugh was a painful, awful sound and he felt tears burn the back of his eyes. He dropped his chin to his chest, glad his father couldn't see his face. "I like Ursula, too. She seems nice."

"No one will ever replace your mother, but this is different. Not more or less, just…different." His dad paused. "It's been nice having someone to spend time with. I've missed that, the companionship."

Finn would miss that too. Just…talking to Meg, being around her, laughing with her. He was going to lose her, only unlike his mother, she hadn't died. She just…didn't want him anymore. That sliced through his soul like razors.

"Have you told her that you love her?" Dad asked.

He glanced over his shoulder, incredulous. As if he was going to discuss that with anyone. So he turned the tables. "Have you? With Ursula?"

Clapping him on the back, Dad chuckled ruefully. "Like father, like son."

"It'll be over when we go back tomorrow," Finn admitted, to himself as much as to his father. What hope did he have left? Meg had been clear about her position before she'd fled to the bathroom.

There was a long moment of silence before his dad spoke again. "If you let her walk away without telling her, you'll regret it. You'll be folding before you've played your trump card, giving up without letting her make a fully informed decision on where you both stand."

"I don't think it'd make a difference." And didn't it rankle to confess that?

"There's only one way to know for sure. Think about it." Dad stepped away, reached into the fridge, and pulled out a frosty bottle of beer. "I think you could use one of these."

Snorting, Finn accepted the offering, popped the top, and took a deep swig. The slightly bitter brew fit his mood perfectly, but it didn't wash away his dad's words. They nagged at him the rest of the evening, through the drive back to the hotel, and on the walk to his room.

He'd come into this thinking he was all-in, that he'd be playing to win, but somehow during this week, he'd started to hold himself back, realizing he might be risking far more than he could afford to lose. His very soul. But she'd taken it anyway. She just didn't know it, and he doubted she'd even want it. And yet...he knew she cared, knew this wasn't a simple fling for her. She wasn't the kind of woman who had simple flings.

Should he tell her the whole truth? Risk everything? If she still left, knowing how he felt, it would gut him. It would be so much worse than saying nothing. But what if knowing he loved her made the difference?

Shaking his head, he pulled out the key card for his room. "Sorry, I forgot to ask if you wanted to stay in my room or yours tonight. I was on autopilot."

"Your room is fine." Tilting her head back, she searched his face, but he had no idea what she'd see there. She gave him a wan smile. "Let's end where we began."

He swallowed back the pain that statement caused. If he had one last night with her, he wanted to take it. Tomorrow was soon enough for regrets and wallowing in the suffering he'd volunteered for.

They walked through the door and he shut it behind them. Her hips swayed as she moved around the room, and he drank in the sight of her. She was so lovely. Everything he'd ever wanted all in one package. Warm, sweet, and sexy.

She looked over at him, her gaze tentative. "I, um, I got you a going away present."

The only present he wanted was for her to forget about going away, but he kept that to himself. "Oh, yeah? Show me."

He expected her to pull something out of her purse, but she tossed her bag on the dresser. Reaching behind her, she unzipped the back of her dress and let it slide down her arms. The garment pooled around her on the floor and she stepped out of it.

His jaw sagged and his erection rose. "Have mercy."

"Is mercy really what you want right now?" She did a little pirouette for him, and he got a full view of her in the skimpiest teddy he'd ever seen. It was made of black lace he could see straight through, the top connected to the bottom by a thin strip of fabric, and a tiny black bow centered between her ripe breasts. The darkness of the lace contrasted with her skin and shadowed the thatch of hair between her legs. Thigh-highs and a pair of black heels completed the erotic ensemble.

The breath wheezed out of his lungs as he tried to find something intelligible to say. "You were wearing that at my father's house?"

"I did feel a little bad about that when I was getting ready, but it's not like I was going to strip during dinner." She approached him, the silk of her stockings whispering as her legs brushed together.

The closer she came, the more his brain seemed to short-circuit. Her nipples thrust into the sheer fabric, and he wanted to suck them. Heat exploded through his veins, made his hands shake with need.

Her fingertips brushed down the ribbon of lace that lay against her stomach. "Do you like it?"

Groaning, he dragged her forward and kissed her hard. His tongue thrust into her mouth, his hands moving to grasp her backside and grind her against his erection. He bit her bottom lip, then licked and nuzzled his way along her jaw and down her throat. She gasped, her hands bunching in his shirt. He took one nipple in his mouth, suckling it through the lace.

A shudder ran through her and she arched her body into him. "Please, Finn."

He offered the same attention to her other breast, his tongue circling the tight tip. Then he bit down, and a low sob spilled out of her. He continued his journey downward, kissing her side, nipping at her navel until he dropped to his knees. Level with her sex, he pressed his face into her. The lace abraded his chin, but he could smell the musky scent of her arousal.

"There are snaps to open the front," she whispered, her fingers threading through his hair.

He glanced up at her, a grin forming on his face. "And you're hoping I use them?"

"God, yes." Her cheeks were rosy, her lips puffy from his kiss, and the look she gave him lit his blood on fire.

A quick jerk opened the snaps and then she was bared to him. Teasing the lips of her sex with his fingertips, he parted her and found that beads of her moisture had dampened her thighs. "So wet for me."

"Yes." Her hands tightened in his hair, urging him forward. "Please, Finn. Please."

There was nothing as sexy as knowing he could make her beg. He couldn't resist her pleas. Not that he wanted to. He dipped one finger into her slick heat, teasing more moisture from her. She whimpered, her hips pushing forward to seek more. He had to taste her. Curling his tongue around her nub, he groaned when her nails dug into him. The flavor of her burst in his mouth—ripe and feminine. He added a second finger to her channel, pumping both into her as he licked and nipped at her sex.

"Oh, God. Yes, yes, yes," she chanted, her breath catching on a little sob.

The way she tugged on his hair made his scalp burn, pain to intensify the experience. He was so hard and hot that he was close to coming in his pants. He pushed her harder, pleasuring her with his hands and mouth. The soft sounds she made told him how near she was to climax. He hooked his finger so it rubbed the spot he knew would make her break. Then he bit her nub.

"Finn!" Her hips jerked, her legs shaking as her inner muscles gripped his fingers in rhythmic pulses.

God, he couldn't wait another second. He had to be inside her. Now. Right this very second. He dragged her to the ground and ripped open his fly. His hands shook as he pulled a condom from his wallet and covered himself. She arched for him, her fingers cupping her breasts while she stared at him in blatant desire.

God, he loved her. Loved to strip all the shyness away until there was only the fiery angel left. He could spend the rest of his life with her and never grow tired of watching her go up in flames. For him. Only for him.

"Hurry, Finn. I want you."

As if he needed the extra incentive. He was over her in moments, surging deep in one sure stroke. They both gave a harsh groan. Her arms and legs twined around him, her hips already undulating beneath him. There was no room for subtlety here—he just pounded into her, his self-control in tatters. Her hand slid under his shirt, her nails digging into his back as she moved with him, her moans driving him even wilder. It was fast and rough, and he rode her hard, grinding his pelvis against her.

Their gazes met, locked. Her need played across her expression, and something tender mingled with it. He loved when she looked at him that way, and his chest tightened with emotion that he had to keep in check. A little smile formed on her lips, and her sex squeezed around his thrusting shaft. It was too much. Grasping the flagging ends of his sanity, he reached between them and thumbed her nub. She froze for one split second, and then screamed as she climaxed. The way her channel milked his length sent him straight over the edge. He came, his body shuddering, and he leaned his forehead against hers, unable to look away, even now.

"I love you." He couldn't hold the words back. His father was right. He had to try.

"I love you, Meg. Stay with me. Don't leave."

Her heart stopped. The breath clogged in her throat and time seemed to stand still. The high of her orgasm crashed and agony stabbed her soul. Why? Why was he doing this to her?

She pushed at his shoulders until he rolled away from her, but the distance between them made her feel so alone, bereft. Choking back a sob, she forced herself to do what she knew was right. "I can't stay with you. You knew that from the beginning. This week was all I ever promised."

"Tell me why." He straightened his clothes, zipping himself back into his pants. His voice was tight when he spoke. "I deserve that, at least."

He deserved a hell of a lot more than that, but she couldn't be the woman to give it to him. "You know why. You knew why before we ever slept together. I've seen how wrong it can go when two teachers date, and I don't want that."

"That's complete bull, Meg. There has to be more to it than that. What we've had in just a few days is better than most relationships I've had...and it's not because I'm bad at relationships, so don't even go there. I'm an *amazing* boyfriend." He crossed his arms, the muscles in his biceps bulging, and the look on his face dared her to contradict him. "So tell me, why? Why are you so bullheadedly against dating another teacher? We aren't those other people who had the big melt-down. I wasn't even here and you weren't the one who got dumped, so why—"

"Because I *was* the one who was dumped." The ugly truth of it ripped out of her throat. Familiar shame and humiliation flooded her.

"What?" His brows dipped together. "No, you weren't. The woman was named Gina or something. I heard all about it after I was hired. Teachers like to gossip."

"Regina, not Gina. Regina and Brandon." She swallowed. "And you heard the version everyone knows."

His gaze sharpened on her, so blue it burned like a laser straight into her soul. "And in the real version, you got dumped instead of Regina?"

"In addition to." Her smile was a mere twitch of the lips. "I... Brandon was my friend. There was a bit of chemistry between us—unspoken, of course, since he and Regina had been together for years before we met. Things were always tempestuous with them. They both liked drama and excitement." This time her lips curved with bittersweet memory. "Brandon came to my apartment one night and told me they'd had a huge fight, that it was over between them. He didn't want to deal with the craziness anymore. We...we had some wine. A lot of it. And one thing led to another...and we..."

"Christ," he breathed.

"It was fine, I thought." She straightened her shoulders, tugging up the strap on the teddy she was wearing. Suddenly the idea of wearing it tonight didn't seem as good as it once had. Pushing to her feet, she went to the bed, picked up a pillow, and hugged it to her chest. "He was available, there'd always been some attraction between us. Now, maybe we could...you know...explore it." Moisture glutted her eyes, but she blinked it away as she sat on the edge of the mattress facing him. "He spent the weekend at my apartment, then went home to start packing his things so he could move out. And move in with me." She rolled her eyes, a tear slipping free. "Because, of course, I was willing to take him in while he got back on his feet."

His throat moved as he swallowed. "Then how did the public melt-down I heard about end up happening?"

"Ah, yes. That." She gritted her teeth to hold in a sob. God, she had to say it. Admit aloud, for the first time ever, just how big a fool she'd been. "So, it took a couple of weeks for him to get his stuff together. He brought a box or two to my place, and told me he was going to put most of his belongings in storage for the time being. He stayed with me most nights, so I didn't have any reason to doubt him. But then..."

"Then?"

She couldn't meet his gaze, so she squeezed her eyes shut. "There was a staff meeting after school one day and Regina confronted him, said she didn't believe him about staying on a friend's couch while they worked stuff out, and accused him of cheating on her. It was ugly."

He drew up a knee and propped his arm on it. "From what I heard, he called her insane, said things were over, and then she attacked him."

"Yep, that about sums it up." She cleared her throat, wishing to be anywhere but here, talking about anything but this. Self-loathing curdled in her belly, and she hated herself for what she'd done three years ago and hated herself even more for what it would cost her now.

Finn.

"So, did he lie to you about breaking up with her in the first place?"

"Or was I an affair that he lied to her about? I'll never know. I'll never know if he turned me into the kind of woman Dad's Barbie was. The bitch who came along, stole someone else's guy, and left a woman humiliated and alone like my mom was." She swallowed the need to vomit. God. It sounded even more horrible when she put it into words. "Regina was fired for assaulting another teacher on school property, and then... I thought when things settled down we could—" She forced herself to finish. "A week after that, the principal let us know that Brandon had resigned effective immediately. He'd given no notice. He'd just quit and walked out. Said he needed to get away from what had happened."

Finn's brow furrowed. "What did he tell you before he left?"

"Nothing. I never saw or heard from him again."

That brought him to his feet. "What the hell?"

"Yes, exactly." She tried to laugh, but her attempt was pathetic. "I kept hoping for a while after that, but...no."

"Jesus." He loomed over her, curling his hand under her chin to make her look at him. "Why didn't Anne say something about this?"

"She doesn't know." She pressed her lips together, jerking her chin out of his grasp. "After everything that had happened...I couldn't tell anyone. What would I say? I may have been a Barbie-like home-wrecker, but I'm not quite sure? I might have caused Regina's mental breakdown by accident? Oops, my bad." She dragged a hand across her eyes. "Or how about a classic? My not-really-boyfriend bailed on me and didn't even leave me a Dear Jane note? How pathetic and disgusting is that? How awful would all that make me?"

"What a douche bag."

She flinched. "At least you're honest."

"Not you, him. Any man who treated two women that way didn't deserve either of them. He should have had the balls to tell both of you he wanted to leave." He sat beside her, catching her shoulders in a hard grip. Fury tightened his face, his jaw turned to iron. "What a spineless douche bag. I'd like to put my fist through his face for doing that to you, Meg. You deserve better."

She shook her head, pushing to her feet. Having his hands on her was too much. It made her want to lean on him, to believe in him—in them—in the possibilities she so desperately wanted but couldn't have. "I just...I can't go through that kind of thing again. Coworkers don't mix. I can't do it."

"I would never do that to you, Meg." He tried to reach for her, but she shrank away from his touch. "I'm not your father or Brandon. I get that your parents left you with some qualms about relationships and then you got tangled up with a guy who reinforced all of your fears, but they are just fears. Life is about taking chances. You can't live it afraid all the time."

"It's not just a fear if you lived through it. Then it's reality." She pressed her hands to her eyes, a small sob shaking her body. "I can't risk going through that again, Finn. I just can't. It's better not to have it at all than to have it and lose it."

"I can't agree with that." Finn's palm curved over the back of her head, and she could feel how desperately he wanted her to believe him. "My mom died and it's not like I run from every woman because she might get breast cancer someday. Hell, even my dad's willing to give a relationship a shot again. People can conquer their fears, Meg, even when those fears are very real. What you and I have is worth fighting for."

"No," she whispered, tears sliding down her cheeks. "Life is about knowing what you can handle and what you can't. And I can't."

And that was the pure, ugly truth. Because things with Finn were so much better, so much more than they had been with Brandon. After only a week. If she let herself get any deeper than this, she couldn't even fathom how bad breaking up with Finn would be a month from now—a year, a decade. She'd be the one forced to leave town if they split up because there was no way she'd be able to face every day of being around him at work and not having him. Losing him could mean losing everything. It was too big of a gamble, too overwhelming to even consider.

Better to cut her losses and run now.

CHAPTER TWELVE

It had killed Finn to see her cry, and he found he couldn't bring himself to push her for what she wasn't ready for. The bottom line was, he was willing to take the risk of a relationship, of the pleasure and pain that came from loving someone.

She was not.

Three weeks later, he had to acknowledge that she might never be ready. There'd been the tiniest thread of hope that she might reconsider once she'd had some time to think. But he had to admit—finally—she wouldn't be able to get over her past. Hell, if he'd dealt with a divorce like her parents', and then a breakup, blowup, and breakdown that made her the same kind of villain she'd hated for shredding her parents' relationship...he'd be gun-shy too. It wasn't as if he didn't understand, but what his brain knew and what his heart felt were two very different things.

At first, he'd been pissed. With her, with fate, with the whole damned world. But he'd learned after his mother died that anger didn't help and would only turn to bitterness. He wasn't willing to let that kind of ugliness consume him, so he'd had to find some acceptance.

The days since his return from Vegas had slipped by, his fury had worn away, and all that was left was missing her. Being without her was like a slow-leaking wound inside of him, a bruise that might never heal. But he had to find a way to get on with his life, even though he'd never have her in it. They'd managed to avoid each other in the weeks they'd been back, and he didn't even want to think about how he'd react when he saw her again. He winced when he realized it would likely be at a staff meeting—something else that was far too close to her experiences with that little pissant bastard Brandon.

Finn shook his head, stuffing a change of clothes into his backpack. It was Friday afternoon and he wanted to get an early start in the morning. He needed to get out of town and clear his mind. A hiking trip in Big Basin sounded perfect. A ninety-minute drive and then two days of quiet solitude in nature with no temptation to go knocking on her door. It was just what he needed now.

A yowl echoed from the bathroom, and then his cat, George, swaggered out and leapt onto the bed, clearly expecting to be petted. Finn snorted and rubbed the feline between his ragged ears. "If you didn't get into so many fights with the other cats in the neighborhood, you wouldn't look so mangy."

Purring with the supreme assurance only cats could manage, George butted his head against Finn's palm. After a few minutes, Finn went back to packing, only to have George constantly get in the way, demanding attention and swiping at Finn when he didn't receive it promptly enough for his liking. Annoyed, Finn finally picked up the tomcat and locked him outside. Getting his gear together had already taken twice as long as it should have.

Once he was packed, he paced the length of his living room. He'd tried TV, but an episode of *Pawn Stars* had been the first thing that came on. He'd flipped to ESPN only to find a college baseball game. Too much reminded him of Meg. He returned to his room so he could change into sweats and some beat-up sneakers. He usually took a run around sunset, then sat on the beach until the final rays disappeared below the horizon. He was running a little earlier than normal, but he'd rather do a couple extra wind sprints than stay here.

After locking his front door, he pocketed his keys and cell phone. A few minutes of stretching on the porch and he was ready to go.

"Hi, Finn."

He glanced over and saw one of his neighbors—a pretty woman who'd always been friendly to him and put cat food out on the porch for George whenever Finn was out of town.

"Oh, hey, Jeannie." The wind picked up and he zipped the front of his hoodie. "How are you?"

"I'm good." Her smile was sunny and welcoming. "Did you have fun on your trip?"

Fun wasn't the word he'd use, but he forced an answering grin. "I did. Thanks for asking. And thanks for looking after my cat."

Not that George liked her. He'd had a hissy fit the one time Jeannie had tried to pet him, but he deigned to allow her to give him food before backing away from the bowl slowly.

"No problem." She hesitated, then seemed to steel herself. "Um...I was wondering if you might like to have coffee sometime."

The request caught him by surprise, and he blinked at her like an idiot. He should do it. Throw himself back out there, and not dwell on his failure with Meg. His neighbor was nice and attractive. And interested in dating him, unlike Meg. He opened his mouth to accept, but that wasn't what came out. "Maybe some other time. I just broke up with—"

"Oh! I'm so sorry, I didn't know." Jeannie's hands fluttered in a flustered gesture. "I just haven't really seen you with any women guests—not that I'm spying on you or anything—oh, crap, this is weird now."

He laughed, the sound straggling past the heaviness that had been pressing down on his chest since Vegas. "It's not weird. Don't worry about it. I'm flattered you asked. It's just bad timing."

"Okay." She managed a brave smile. "See you later."

"Later." He waved, and then turned for the Pacific.

Another example of his mind and heart not being on the same page. His mind said move on, his heart wasn't there yet. He still loved Meg too much to pretend he was ready to try again with someone else. He stretched his legs into a run when he hit the sand and concentrated on regulating his breathing as the ocean waves lapped at the beach. It hurt like hell to be without Meg now, but it wouldn't always be that way. He might always wonder what might have been, but he would heal, and Vegas would eventually be a bittersweet memory.

He'd be all right, someday.

H ugo nudged her hand, whimpering in that sad, pathetic way of his, giving Meg the big puppy dog eyes. It was hard to say which of them was more depressed and miserable. She'd been putting on a good face at work, but alone at home she could admit it. Classes had been back in session for three whole weeks, and she'd done everything in her power to avoid seeing Finn. It wouldn't last. The school—hell, the town—wasn't that big, and she'd have to deal with him eventually.

It just hurt. All the time, every single second. Doing the right thing shouldn't make her feel so awful, but it did. She wrapped an afghan around herself and curled up on her couch, closing her eyes. Hugo gave a wheezy grunt as he heaved himself onto the sofa with her and laid his head across her ankles.

A knock sounded on her door, and she ignored it. She didn't want to see or talk to anyone. It was Friday and she had the whole weekend to wallow in her self-pity and pretend the world didn't exist. She'd been doing that for three weekends straight and she was starting to annoy herself, but she hadn't been able to muster up the energy to care enough to change anything.

The front doorknob rattled and she heard the hinges creak as the door swung open. Aw, damn. Her friends had keys to her place, and now she was going to pay for ignoring their calls and skipping their weekly dinners. She hadn't even managed to sit up before they ranged around her, arms folded across their chests.

"You've been avoiding us," Julie accused.

"It's not just you." Meg pushed her hair out of her face. "I don't feel well. Go away."

"It's been three weeks, so either you're dying or you're lying." Karen sat on the coffee table, crossing her legs.

Anne snorted, jerking the blanket away from Meg. "We're staging an intervention. Get your purse and grab the dog."

For about half a second she considered protesting and then gave it up for a lost cause. It would be faster to just go along with whatever they wanted so she could come home and get back to stewing in her wretchedness. Sighing, she pushed herself to her feet, put on some shoes, and fetched her purse and a leash for Hugo. She clipped it on his collar. "Come on, buddy. Your aunts want to torture you."

They all piled into Karen's sedan—Julie, Meg and Hugo stuffed into the back. Julie scratched one of the dog's ears. "He really is the saddest specimen of a mutt on the planet."

Karen chortled and regaled them with a few more stories of Hugo versus her husband. Tate didn't seem to have fared well in the battles and Karen was a little too gleeful about it. Meg closed her eyes and pressed her forehead against the window. They were making idle conversation now, but the grilling would commence soon enough and she had to figure out what to say.

They hit a speed bump and her eyes flew open. She'd figured they were going to dinner at the Moonside Café, but they'd turned right toward the ocean instead of left toward town. "Where are we going?"

Karen glanced in the rearview mirror and met her gaze. "We thought we'd go for a walk on Poplar Beach. Is that okay?"

Reeling in Hugo's leash, Meg nodded. "Sure."

A few more speed bumps and they were in the parking lot near the beach. They climbed out and Anne and Karen went to handle the parking meter. Julie and Meg sat on the hood of the car to wait for their friends. The ocean dominated the view, but they'd have to walk down a bluff to get to the beach.

Julie propped her elbows on her knees. "Anne told us about Finn, how he asked her to talk you in to Vegas. We're assuming you guys hooked up there, it didn't go well, and that's why you've been sick with the plague for weeks."

"It's not his fault." No, it was all her fault. Finn had been amazing about everything. He wasn't perfect, but he'd fit her so well. He made her laugh. Her lips twisted.

Julie's gaze was sympathetic. "So, you ended it and not him, huh? Anne hasn't been able to pry any more out of him than we've gotten out of you. It might help to talk about it."

Maybe, but to explain what had gone wrong with Finn would mean admitting to what had gone wrong with Brandon. That she might have been the Other Woman. That the idea of misjudging a man that badly again had kept her from even trying with Finn. Tears glutted her eyes, as they had far too many times in the last few weeks.

Karen came up on the other side of her, settling on the car. "Come on, tell us what happened. You don't want to make us do this the hard way."

A tearful chuckle trickled out of her. She doubted the truth would set her free, but at least she wouldn't be troubled by the lies anymore. There was something to be said for that. "Okay. I need to tell you guys some stuff that happened a few years ago."

Julie held her hand while the truth spilled out, Karen slid a supporting arm around her waist, and Anne paced in front of them, a protective mother hen ready to attack. Hugo just sat there and looked worried, whining and nosing Meg's shoes. It took a while to get it all out—to admit everything. She felt like a fool all over again—somehow, she doubted that royal screwup would ever stop burning a hole in her belly.

She hunched her shoulders. "I'm sorry I didn't say anything. At first, I thought he'd come back. I was so stupid. And the longer I waited, the stupider I felt." She clenched her teeth to keep her lips from shaking. "The more I realized Regina might have been right and he may have been cheating on her with me."

"Oh, hon. With your parents' breakup, that had to have been the worst part." Karen hugged her closer, and Meg shuddered with a sob.

"It should have occurred to me, but I didn't even consider that he'd lie to me. I should have known better and learned from my mother's example." She leaned on Karen's shoulder. "I was such an idiot."

"Yeah, you were," Anne said bluntly, still pacing back and forth. "Not because of that jackass, but because we're friends and we would have been there for you. That's the kind of time when you need friends the most."

"I know." Meg sighed, though she did feel better not having to keep this from them anymore. Nothing had changed, but she felt unburdened. A small improvement. "You're right and I'm sorry. I'm sorry about pretty much everything I did back then."

"Don't be." Julie squeezed her hand. "We all make mistakes."

"Did the week in Vegas with Finn bring this up?" Anne asked, her hair ruffling in a fiery halo when the sea breeze kicked up.

Meg rubbed her eyes. "Yes."

"What are you going to do about him?" Julie put in.

"I don't know. He says he loves me." Her tongue tripped over the word. Brandon had told her the same thing and that hadn't made him stick around when things got rough, had it? And Finn hadn't spoken to her since they got back from spring break. She knew that wasn't fair—she hadn't spoken to him either. And why would he want to talk to her? *She'd* been the one to push him away and demand a return to their former distance.

"Do you love him? Because it doesn't matter what he feels if you don't feel the same way. A relationship based on sex isn't worth it and won't last." The bitter tinge to Karen's words made Meg wonder if she was speaking from experience.

"There was definitely sex, but it wasn't like we spent the whole week in bed. And it's not like we didn't know each other before. It was more than just sex. A lot more." Saying that aloud was painful, because she hadn't been able to admit her feelings to Finn. She liked him, respected him, and she knew he liked and respected her.

He loved her.

"But do you love him?" Karen persisted, pushing a stray lock of blond hair behind her ear. "Or...could you fall in love with him if you let yourself?"

Ah, there was the rub. The question she absolutely hadn't allowed herself to face. "I love him, but I am so scared. Of ending up like Mom and Dad, or Brandon and me. There are no guarantees."

"Nope." Julie slid off the hood and pushed away from the car. "Relationships are a risk. So, you have to ask yourself if you trust yourself to make the right decision this time, and if you trust him to stick by you, even though your dad and Brandon were faithless jerks." She glanced back. "No offense to your dad, but..."

"Those weren't his best moments," Meg finished. "He's apologized to me and to Mom, but that doesn't change what he did."

She sat there for a long time, silent. Did she trust Finn not to bail on her? Not to cheat and hurt her? Did she trust her own judgment well enough to be willing to make a commitment to him? That was probably the worst of Brandon's crimes, in the end. Not that he'd lied and left her, but that his actions had destroyed her faith in herself. And she'd let him do it. That seared her soul. She'd let him steal her chance to be happy with someone else. She'd let him make her afraid.

But she'd grown since then. She had taken a risk on Finn. Maybe not the biggest risk of all—commitment—but she'd gotten involved with a colleague. That had been a huge step. She'd been a lot more spontaneous when she was with him, willing to react without over-analyzing everything. She had changed, little by little. It felt as if she'd been hiding inside a protective shell for years, only coming out of it for her friends, and Finn had made her want to free herself from it entirely. When had the protection become a prison?

It wouldn't be the end of the world to go out on a date with him. It wasn't as if she had to marry him tomorrow. If things didn't work out, she'd be hurt, and that hurt would take a long time to get over. She had to accept that possibility too—the good and the bad. But wasn't she hurting now? Wasn't she regretting the missed chance with Finn? Did she want to feel like this every time she ran into him at work? Maybe it would get better with time, but did she want it to? Did she want to feel good about chickening out on what might have been perfect for her?

No. No, she didn't want to take the coward's way out. She didn't want to doubt herself forever, too scared to go after what she wanted and fight to keep it. She believed in herself enough to do this, and she believed in Finn enough to know he wouldn't hurt her on purpose. There were still no guarantees that they'd live happily ever after, but...she had to at least try.

"Hey, look at this, guys."

She blinked and saw Anne motioning them over to the edge of the bluff. The group straggled over to join her, with Meg tugging Hugo's leash to get the hound moving. It took her a moment to see what Anne was pointing at, and when she did, her stomach did a backflip. A tall man was running short sprints back and forth on the beach, his hair gleaming red in the sunset.

"Finn." She turned an accusing gaze on Anne. "You knew he'd be here."

"Guilty as charged." Her friend leaned in close. "What are you going to do about it?"

"I'm not ready to see him." She stumbled back a step. Sure, she'd decided to find out if he still wanted to date her, but talking to him about it right this second was terrifying.

"Nobody's ready for love," Karen retorted, the voice of experience. "That doesn't really stop it from showing up."

"You can't hide forever." Julie bumped her shoulder against Meg's. "What you had with Brandon wasn't real because he wasn't genuine."

"Finn is," Anne finished. "Don't compound your first mistake by making an even bigger one now. He loves you, and he's been a nasty beast to work with the last couple of weeks. So be a pal and put me out of his misery."

Meg laughed, the sound watery.

"All right." Karen made a shooing motion at the other two. "We've done all we can. It's up to you if you want to go down and talk to him."

Julie ruffled Meg's hair. "We'll be at the Moonside. It's a short walk if you decide you want to join us instead of talking to him. We're here for you no matter what."

And they would be there for her if Finn decided he didn't want to deal with her fears. Which he had every right to do, especially after she'd kicked him out of her life. It was a comfort, knowing her girls would always be on her side. She should have told them about Brandon a long time ago. If she hadn't bottled it up all these years, she might have gotten over it by now. She put that regret aside. Beating herself up over the past hadn't helped, and she needed to look forward, not back. "Thanks."

Anne leaned in for a quick hug, and whispered in Meg's ear, "You're not going to find one like him again, hon. Don't throw away happiness."

"I won't," she whispered back. "Let's just hope he still wants me."

"He does." Anne's smile held the confidence Meg lacked.

She'd put him through the ringer, rejected the love he'd offered her. It seemed only fair she give him the opportunity to return the favor. Queasiness settled in her belly as her friends drove away. She really despised confrontation—a trait picked up from watching her parents argue—and now she was in for the fight of her life. God, help her.

"Come on, Hugo."

He gave a whining little grunt as he heaved to his feet and followed her down the trail to the beach. The walk across the sand seemed endless. Finn was a blur, he ran so fast. He'd stop just long enough to touch the wet beach, then shoot in the other direction for about fifty feet and do the same thing. A churned furrow showed he'd been at it for a while. He didn't even glance up as she drew near, his brow creased in concentration.

"Finn."

He stumbled as she spoke, whipping around to stare at her as if she were a ghost. Chest heaving, sweat pouring down his skin, he swiped a hand across his face. "Meg."

"Hi." She tried not to cringe at her own banality.

He glanced around at the deserted beach. "What are you doing here?"

Courage, Meg. Courage. He'd said what they had was worth fighting for, and she had to believe he meant it. "I came to talk to you. Anne gave me a push in the right direction."

That earned a snort. "I hope it wasn't too hard a push."

"Just enough to get me moving." Her lips twisted. "It's good to see you."

"It hurts to see you."

The frank words made tears burn her eyes, but she blinked them back. She deserved whatever he had to dish out. "I want to apologize."

He glanced away. "You don't need to do that."

"Yes, I do." She pulled Hugo a bit closer, until she stood right in front of Finn and looked him straight in the eye. "I love you. And I need to apologize for being too gutless to admit it before now. I need to apologize for hurting you and leaving you."

"I knew when we started our affair that I might not come out of it unscathed." His blue gaze was hooded, and whatever reaction he'd had to her declaration of love remained hidden.

This was not going well. The queasiness in her stomach made bile burn its way up her throat, but she refused to back down. "I want another chance, if you're still interested. Maybe we could have dinner or coffee or something."

He sighed, closed his eyes and swallowed. "Meg, I don't know. It would kill me if you changed your mind again."

"I won't." She edged closer, dared to lay her hand on his chest, felt the warmth and vitality of him beneath his sweatshirt. "History is my specialty, but in this case, dwelling on the past didn't serve me well at all. I've been running scared for a long time, pretending that I was just being logical about my relationship choices, and you made me stop and question why I was doing all of that. Yanking someone out of a rut is usually uncomfortable for everyone concerned, and you didn't exactly see me at my best." She licked her lips, and she watched his eyes follow her movements. Heat flared in his gaze before he banked it, but it gave her some hope. "I didn't treat you very well and I wasn't entirely honest with you. I'd like the chance to change that."

"What makes you think this will go better than it did last time?"

It was a fair question. She'd spent the last year holding him at arm's length because dating a colleague was a mistake that would end badly. "Because you were right. You're not Brandon, I'm not the woman I was when I was with him, and I think you're twice the man he could ever hope to be. You would never treat a woman the way he did or the way my father did my mother, and I think if you weren't happy with a relationship, you'd be adult enough to bow out of it instead of straying."

His gaze darkened, and she could see his inner turmoil. "You know, I'd given up on you."

"Don't." Her heart clutched, pain slicing through her. She balled her hands in his sweatshirt, a tear escaping the corner of her eye. "Don't give up on me, please."

"Meg." His hand lifted to cup her cheek, wiping the moisture away.

"You love me, and I love you." She laid her forehead against his chest, willing him to listen to her, to believe her. "We can make this work, I know it. We don't even have to make any kind of commitments now. Just agree to have dinner. We can go really slowly, if you want."

"I don't think that will work for me." His hands closed over her shoulders, holding her away from him.

She gritted her teeth to keep in a sob, but she couldn't stop another tear from escaping. "Please reconsider, Finn. I promise I'll do better this time. I'd be an awesome girlfriend, if you'd let me."

A faint smile curved his lips. "I meant that taking it slowly and not making commitments wouldn't work for me."

"Oh. Oh." Joy broke through her as what he'd said finally processed. Her heart skipped a beat, then raced.

His fingers dug into her shoulders. "I would want you to be my awesome girlfriend. Publicly."

It was a test. One she had to pass. It was scary, but he wasn't a man for half-measures. Either she was in or she was out. She swallowed and nodded. "Okay. I'm willing if you are."

"Are you sure?"

"Very. I'm not going to change my mind." She hated the doubt in his gaze. Reaching up, she cupped her hand on his jaw. "I love you, Finn. Making you stick to our bargain had nothing to do with how I felt about you and everything to do with my fears. You were right about that. You were right about everything." She let out a shaky breath. "I had to work through a lot of stuff, and I probably have more to work through. I'm hoping you'll help me with that. But believe that I love you. I don't think anyone will ever fit me as well as you do."

His throat worked. "I love you, too. Don't ever leave me again."

"I won't. I promise. I can be very tenacious when I want to be, you know."

"Oh, I know." Then a smile broke across his face, tender and wicked and exactly the way she remembered. "Let's just promise to always be honest with each other, no matter how difficult the truth might be. I think that's how we make sure we don't end up where we don't want to be."

"Deal." It sounded like the best plan she'd ever heard. She could see love shining in his gaze and knew everything was going to be all right. "Kiss me?"

His fingers threaded through her hair, and he brushed his lips over her forehead, her cheek, the tip of her nose, her jaw, her chin, before settling on her mouth. It was sweet and hot at the same time, hungry and reverent. Perfect. He parted her lips with his tongue, and she twined hers with his. His hands streaked down her back as if relearning her shape. He cupped her backside, pulling her tight to his hard body. Need filtered through her, rising like a slow tide, but for now she was content to kiss him, love him.

God, she loved him.

She threw her arms around his neck, and a canine yelp of pain brought her back down to earth. She still had Hugo's leash in her hand and she'd yanked it too hard. Bending down, she stroked a palm over his head. "Sorry, buddy."

He flopped down onto the sand, the picture of despondence.

"Wow, he really is a depressive mutt." Finn knelt beside her, scratching the dog behind one ear.

She spread her hands. "I know, right? I swear I don't abuse him. He's spoiled rotten."

"Come on. I know a great spot to sit and watch the sunset. Even Hugo here will like it." The corners of his eyes crinkled as he stood and proffered a hand. "Then we can head back to my place for a more private reunion."

She slipped her fingers into his and let him help her to her feet. "That sounds just right. And tomorrow you'll let me take you out to dinner at the Moonside."

His eyebrows arched. "Go big or go home. I like it."

"I thought you might." It was about as public a statement as she could make short of taking an ad out in the local paper. Everyone knew her at that restaurant, and tongues would definitely start wagging.

Good. Let them. She knew what she wanted, and she didn't care if everyone else knew it too. No more hiding, no more allowing the past to rob her of the future she wanted.

What do you know? The truth really had set her free.

THE END

Want more from C. Jordan? Sign up for her newsletter:
https://www.cjordanbooks.com/newsletter

ABOUT C. JORDAN

C. Jordan is a California native with an insatiable love for travel. When she's not writing sexy contemporary romance, she can usually be found working as a librarian or wandering the world with her husband.

ALSO BY C. JORDAN

EXCERPT FROM NEVER LET GO

Half Moon Bay, California

"Julie?" Karen called from the front of the shop. "Julie, where are you?"

"In the back." A bittersweet sensation swamped Julie as she gazed around Purl Moon Fiber Arts. Wooden shelves held stacks of every imaginable color and fiber of yarn—a beautiful, touchable rainbow. An old-fashioned spinning wheel dominated one corner, and the basket beside it contained a long braid of roving wool just waiting to be spun. It was the last batch of wool she'd hand-died with her great-aunt. She hadn't been able to make herself finish it.

Tears stung her eyes, but a smile curled her lips. Damn, she missed Auntie Eloise. The feisty old woman had taught Julie to knit and crochet in this very shop. She'd learned to spin on that wheel. Lovely memories.

"Here you are." Karen came around one of the display shelves. "Are you ready?"

Reaching over, Julie unplugged the lights on the miniature Christmas tree. Crocheted snowflake decorations graced every branch, most of them Auntie's creations. Putting up the tree had always been something Julie and Eloise did together, but this year she was on her own. It was too much, too painful. She'd held it together during the worst of the holiday shopping rush, but it was four days before Christmas and she was closing up and getting out of town. She just couldn't bear it.

Clearing her throat, she turned to her friend. "Ready as I'll ever be. Is Tate with you?"

Karen's face fell a little before she pasted on a wide grin. "He couldn't make it, but he said to tell you happy holidays and have fun. He's busy with work today."

And every other day, but Julie didn't say it. Things weren't golden in Karen's marriage, which was a shame. Julie liked Tate, always had, but he was a workaholic who wasn't giving his wife what she needed. If things didn't improve soon, she wasn't sure what would happen, but the shadows in Karen's eyes said she was reaching the end of her tolerance.

Stepping forward, Julie gave her friend a hug. They both could use one right now. It had been a rough year. "Hang in there, sweetie."

Karen squeezed her tight. "You too."

The bell jangled over the shop door. Anne shouted, "Are you two about done? Meg's out here worrying about Julie missing her flight! You know how I hate listening to Meg nag. Get a move on!"

"I'm coming, I'm coming!" Julie rolled her eyes and let Karen go. She pointed to a big suitcase, her purse propped on top. "Grab my bags, will you?"

"Sure."

A quick check of Purl Moon showed the windows and doors were closed and locked. She switched off the lights, set the security system and motioned Karen ahead of her. Once they'd exited, she secured the deadbolt on the front door.

Cool air wrapped around her, the salty hint of the Pacific Ocean curling into her nose. Tidy little shops like hers ran up and down Main Street, looking like a scene from a postcard, all festooned with Christmas lights and wreaths to celebrate the season. A season Julie wanted to escape.

"It's about time you got out of town," Anne barked. "You need a vacation."

"Well, what do you think the baggage is for?" Julie winked at her friend, who stuck out her tongue in return.

Julie watched Anne wrestle the enormous suitcase she was taking to Hawaii into the back of a subcompact car. She wasn't sure how the other woman managed that feat of engineering, but she wasn't about to question it either. Anne was tall, wiry, athletic, and as sarcastic as she was opinionated. Even luggage and the laws of physics bowed before her tenacity.

The four of them—Meg, Julie, Anne, and Karen—had been a tight-knit group since elementary school. Julie was grateful for their friendship, but never more so than the last year. They'd been a solid support as Julie watched her great-aunt's health fade. They'd all been there in the hospital with her when Auntie Eloise had passed.

Hot grief poured through Julie, making her clench her fists at her sides. It wasn't fair. Eloise had still been so *alive*, so active. She'd run her own business right up until she'd had a series of small strokes that had left her struggling to walk and speak clearly. Julie had been living in San Francisco at the time, working as an office manager, but she'd come back to help out, taking over Purl Moon until the spunky old lady could get back on her feet.

It had never happened.

Two months later, a massive stroke had stolen Auntie Eloise's life. Over. Done. Gone. Just that quickly. Julie tried to tell herself that Eloise had lived a long, full life, that she'd had a lot of years to do all the things she enjoyed. But it didn't help much. It still just *hurt*.

"I'm really glad you're getting a break. You need it, honey." Meg walked up with a carrying container filled with two cups of coffee from a café across the street. She glanced at Karen. "Finn's saving us a table for when we finally get rid of these girls."

"Oh, *loverboy*," Anne sang out. "I hooked you guys up, don't forget it. You'd still be giving him a case of blue balls if it weren't for me."

Julie had to bite her lip to keep from chortling like an immature teenager. Karen rocked back on her heels, her green eyes dancing with mirth.

"How could anyone forget your act of daring in convincing me to have a wild week in Vegas? My hero. I'll have Finn start writing thank you cards every time he gets some. Just to show how happy he is to be less blue." Meg sighed dramatically before she handed the liquid ambrosia to Julie, then popped open the passenger door of Anne's car to set the remaining cup in the console. When she straightened and their eyes met, there was enough sympathy in her friend's gaze to make Julie's throat tighten, and any urge to laugh died away. Meg said softly, "It'll be good for you to have some time to yourself."

"You should hook up with a nice Hawaiian cabana boy. Get him to teach you the hula...in bed." Anne slammed the trunk closed and did a bad imitation of the hula, with a less than subtle bump-and-grind move thrown in.

"Oh Jesus. Don't ever do that in public again." Karen shook her head. "And you teach impressionable children."

"It is amazing they let me loose around kids, isn't it?" Anne ruffled a hand over her shock of red hair.

Julie tightened the belt on her coat and gave Meg a look. "Are you sure you and Finn want to do Christmas with her?"

"Her, her three whacky sisters, and her drama mama, you mean?" Meg waggled her eyebrows and brushed an unruly curl away from her face. The cold, misting winter rain did nothing to help her tame her hair. "We'll survive. Probably."

Julie wrapped each of her friends in a quick hug before sliding into the car. Karen held the door for her and shut it after Julie drew her legs in. She heard Karen's muffled voice through the glass. "Okay, Anne. Try not to kill anyone on the way to the airport. Auto accidents make for bad vacation starters."

Bouncing into the driver's seat, Anne pushed the button to roll down the passenger window and leaned across Julie to blow a raspberry at Meg and Karen. "For the record, I am a fantastic driver, and my family is *awesome* during the holidays. We put the fun in dysfunctional."

The four of them burst into giggles before Anne gunned her little car down Main Street. It felt good to laugh. Julie hadn't done enough of it lately. Anne had offered to have Julie over for the dysfunctional fun, but she needed to get out of Half Moon Bay. She needed to get away from anything that reminded her of Aunt Eloise. Honolulu was just the ticket. A week of lounging on the beach sipping cocktails sounded like heaven right now. No worries, no stress. A little grin tugged at her mouth. Who knew? Maybe she'd even find some nice cabana boy to teach her the hula...in bed.

www.ingramcontent.com/pod-product-compliance
Lightning Source LLC
Chambersburg PA
CBHW020010140726
47904CB00018B/2203